CU00641446

HUNGRY WOLF

AN ALPHA WOLVES LOVE CURVES NOVEL

AIDY AWARD

FREE BOOK

Need more curvy girls getting their happy ever afters?

I got you covered!

Join my Curvy Connection newsletter! and I'll send you an exclusive book not for sale anywhere as a gift from me to you!

—> geni.us/CurvyConnection

You'll get book release news, contests and giveaways, and exclusive previews and excerpts. I'll send you another curvy girl romance book just to say thanks! You can even join my review team and get the next book before it's even released.

THIS WOLF IS HUNGRY...AND HE KNOW JUST WHICH THIGHS HE WANTS TO BITE~

This wolf is hungry...and he know just which thighs he wants to bite~

Aleksei is too damaged to fall in love or for anyone to love him. No brave wolftress would want to be mated to the enforcer who couldn't save their alpha from being assassinated. The last thing he needs is to be set up by the matchmaking widow of the man whose life he failed to protect, at a Friendsgiving dinner with their whole family, and at a strip club, none the less. What he needs is a decoy date to get everyone off his back.

Helena has purposefully pushed love away anytime it even looks at her funny. She won't be burned like that again. She's even gone so far as to get the one job in town that would keep men off her back. No one is going to make a pass at the plus-size manager of the Naughty Wolf gentleman's club. Except the town's matchmaker doesn't buy any of it. Now Helena's goal is to get through Friendsgiving without appearing like a pathetic loser who doesn't have anyone to love them. What she needs is one of those growly Troika boys to act as her date just for one night.

Hungry Wolf is a holiday fake relationship story about a broken hero and a sassy curvy girl set in the Wolves Want

Curves world where you'll get to revisit all your favorite characters again.

For the Amazeballs~

I love me some pie.

— DEAN WINCHESTER

NAUGHTY LADIES

*H*elena surveyed her new office in the back of the Naughty Wolf and pinched herself just to make sure it was all real.

Ouch.

Yep. She wasn't dreaming and she was going to have a bruise on the back of her hand. That was okay. It wasn't like the kind of guys who came to a gentlemen's club were looking at her hands. She'd take that mark all day, every day, twice on Sundays, if it meant this new life she'd built was real.

Kosta had given her this big fat promotion and it was exactly the break she needed. Sure, she made good money dancing. Despite what society and her ex might think, her plus-size ass was in high demand for lap dances among the gentleman who frequented the club. But getting promoted to manager meant she had a whole lot more job stability. She got a cut of the whole club's take each night and that meant she'd finally be able to pay off the mountain of debt her jackass ex had left her with.

A gaggle of giggles sounded from the hallway, breaking the silence of the empty club. Helena frowned. She'd come in early for her first day as manager and hadn't expected any of the girls to come in for hours.

"Helena, we brought champagne to celebrate your promotion." Daphine, Debbie Joy, Heather, Kerrie, and Michelle stuck their heads in through the office door. Daphine held an inexpensive bottle in the air and Michelle waved some plastic flutes at her.

Despite her best efforts to be all business, her mouth turned up in a warm smile at them. The other dancers at the club were the closest she had to friends besides Heli. "Come on in, girly-girls, and pour me a glass. I should have known you wouldn't let me actually get any work done."

"Really? Awesome." The five ladies looked at each other like they were surprised Helena was down for celebrating. They half-fell into the room and plunked down on any available flat surface.

The champagne cork popped, and the wine and gossip flowed. "Of course we're not going to let you work. You already work too hard."

Helena took her glass of bubbles and took a sip to appease the girls. "Yeah, keeping your butts out of trouble."

Debbie Joy turned her yoga-pants-clad butt cheek toward Helena and slapped it. "No, that's what the bouncers are for. Has anyone else noticed how every single dude Kosta gets to work here is, like, ultra good-looking?"

Everyone nodded. Heather sighed and looked all dreamy. "Yeah...and built."

"Not to mention hung like an elephant." Kerrie waggled her eyebrows.

Michelle faux gasped. "Wait. How do you know that? Oooh. Are you sleeping with a bouncer?"

Helena let the girls have their fun for a few more minutes. She'd shoo them away in a bit so she could dig into the mountain of paperwork Kosta had left her. He was giving her a whole hell of a lot of responsibility and she intended to earn her keep. Neither Kosta nor Heli were around as much anymore since they'd taken on the project of restoring the Inn at the Bay.

Out of all the employees of the Naughty Wolf, she alone knew the real reason her boss and best friend spent all their time down at the Bay. These ladies with all their giggles and gossip had no idea the bouncers were all actually something more than well-built, sexy, hot tough guys.

So much more.

If she hadn't seen Kosta turn into a wolf with her own eyes, she probably still wouldn't believe it. Since that day it was so obvious to her which men in their little town had the beast inside of them, and which didn't. The wolf pack guys had this innate confidence, an easy and relaxed swagger that she found a little too enticing.

Which was a bad thing. She was not going there. Not with any man or wolf. She was perfectly fine on her own, thank you very much.

Daphine topped off everyone's glasses. "So, Helena. Now that you're in charge, we have a favor to ask."

Uh-oh. Helena looked around the circle at the hopeful, expectant faces. Crap. What did they want from her?

Michelle snort-laughed. "Don't look at us like we're going to ask you for your first-born child. We just want to know if you would host Thanksgiving here this year. None of us has family around."

"Or if we do, we aren't spending an entire freaking day with them." Heather rolled her eyes and then her head, like spending time with her family induced a demonic possession or at least a painful kink in the neck.

Kerrie shrugged. "We want to spend it with the people here, they're the family we choose, you know?"

Ah. Helena did know. While she did her best to keep men at arm's length, the women at the club were more important to her than any imagined mom or sisters she'd never had, and getting kicked out of the house at seventeen didn't exactly make her feel warm and fuzzy toward her puritanical father. Holidays were never very big in their house.

"You didn't have to bribe me with champagne to ask that. I'm happy for all of us to have Thanksgiving dinner here. I'll even bring the pie." It would be nice to share a meal and talk about what they were grateful for.

"And a date," Debbie Joy said, folding her arms.

Not this again. They were eternally on her to find a man. "What? No. That would be one more person to split the pie with."

Suddenly all eyes were on her like she'd just fallen flat on her face on stage. Kerrie folder her arm and slumped into an exaggerated pout. "We never get to meet your boyfriends."

"That's because she doesn't have any," Daphine jibed.

Kerrie, who was newer to their made-up little family, grimaced. "Oops. Sorry. We'd like to meet your girlfriend."

Daphine gave Kerrie a shove. "That's not what I meant."

Another woman stuck her head in the office. "What's this I hear about a Thanksgiving dinner?"

"Selena, hi. We were just talking about having dinner here for the employees after we close on Thursday. You don't think Kosta will mind, will he?"

"Well, I just love the idea. I was on my way here to see if anyone wanted to come up to my house, but this sounds like a whole lot more fun. You don't mind if I crash, do you?"

What, like they were going to say no to the owner's mother? "Of course you can come too."

"Oh goodie. I'll tell the boys we're having dinner here. Shall we do potluck style? I have just the man to set you up with for dinner, Helena. You're going to simply love him. I already have several heritage turkeys thawing in the fridge. Lots of meat eaters in my family, you know. I'm sure Heli is going to want to go overboard on pies. Mmm. Pie. I'll just set up a quick Google Doc for everyone to sign up to say what they're bringing. I'll email you all in a few minutes. I can't wait to meet your young gentlemen, ladies. See you all on Thursday." Selena walked back out of the office, tapping away on her phone screen.

Mouths hung open, eyes stared wide, and the five of them waited silently for a full minute until they heard the back door open and then close. Debbie Joy was the first one to regain her mouth to brain coordination. "Wait. What just happened? Did we just get steamrolled into having Thanksgiving dinner with the Troikas?"

"Yep." Helena took a big gulp of her champagne.

Heather automatically refilled the glass. "And did she say she's setting you up on a blind date?"

Sigh. Helena drained every last dribble of the bubbles. "I was hoping I'd imagined that."

Crap. Helena did not need a date. How the hell was she going to get out of this one?

She'd just have to develop a case of the clumsies and spill her pie all over his pants before dinner even started. No, pie was too precious, especially if it came from The Sleepy Folk's pie shop. Gravy. Yeah, perfect. Brown gravy from sternum to crotch would send any unwanted date running.

It would be so much better if she could figure out a way to get out of the date in the first place, though, so the poor slob Selena wanted to set her up with didn't have to suffer a mashed potato and gravy fate.

Hmm. Did she feel a sore throat coming on?

No. No she did not. Ugh. Even if she did, Selena and the girls would probably come drag her out of bed, pretty her up, and drag her butt to the dinner anyway.

Oh, oh, oh. What if they didn't close the club that night and the dinner had to be hosted somewhere else? No, the Naughty Wolf was never open on holidays. Kosta insisted the staff have time off and even usually gave them all bonuses. He wouldn't keep it open just because Helena told him to, even if she was his new manager.

Fine. She was back to the gravy plan. She'd sign up to provide very hot, like boiling, gravy for the dinner and spill it right on any guy she didn't recognize who walked through the door on Thursday evening.

"Helena," Daphine's tone was much too close to parental. "What are you plotting?"

"Nothing. Only thinking about what dish to bring." Which was one-hundred percent true.

"I think we'd better relegate you to rolls, otherwise

you're liable to spill a perfectly good green bean casserole on some poor unsuspecting schmoe."

"I would never..." She was so busted, and totally screwed.

Not even in the fun way. Not that she even remembered what that felt like.

Whatever. She had a couple of days to figure out how to get out of this blind date. No way was she going to let her Friendsgiving be ruined by a random dude.

THE SET UP

*A*leksei sat in the dark of his small cabin on the edge of Troika land, sipping on a tumbler of vodka. It wasn't like the alcohol had enough punch to get him drunk. He simply liked the burn.

Nothing torched his gut like the knowledge that he alone had let his entire pack down. He should have died that day protecting his Alpha. Not run back home like a scared puppy with his tail tucked between his legs.

The bastards had almost killed him. The taste of the poison fed both to him and Piotr by those fucking Crescent one-bloods lingered with every bite of food he ate, every sip of drink he took. If Niko hadn't already destroyed the bastards and taken over their pack, the need for revenge would still ache in Aleksei's soul.

Now that pain and darkness had nowhere to go. He sat, day after day, waiting for an assignment from any of the Troikas that would make him feel useful again, show them that he wasn't a liability to the pack. None came.

Not that long ago, Aleksei was the greatest Enforcer the

Troika pack had. Now he was their weakest link. They thought him so fragile they didn't even assign him the simplest of jobs. Ever since Kosta had discovered the ring trafficking human women for the benefit of one-bloods, he had enforcers acting as bouncers at The Naughty Wolf. Security beefed up their presence all over Rogue, and the surrounding areas that were controlled by the Troikas.

They told Aleksei to rest up, but he knew what was really going on. They didn't trust him anymore. He was the one wolf who could have saved their father and he'd failed. Failed them all. Failed himself.

Now he was nothing more than a burden on the pack.

That, he couldn't allow. Tonight, he would go lone. A wolf without a pack was the lowest of their society. It was exactly where he belonged.

Aleksei tossed back the remaining vodka and smashed the glass against the cold fireplace. He stood and shook out his limbs that were sore and tired from doing nothing for far too long. Slowly he unbuttoned his flannel shirt and let it drop to the ground.

He barely felt as if he had the right to take on his true wolf form, but it was his only remaining solace.

His pants followed his shirt onto the ground, then his socks, and finally his t-shirt. His wolf was always near the surface these days and Aleksei welcomed the snap of bones and the painful reforming of his shape that came with the transformation. His claws burst from the end of his fingers first, then his fangs dropped from his gums.

The wolf inside growled low at a noise outside the cabin and wanted nothing more than to tear the intruder apart.

"Who is there?" His voice came out more beast than man and he sniffed the air.

He caught the scent of the last person on the face of the Earth he wanted to see. Selena, Piotr's widow and the pack's former matriarch. She had been too kind to him in the months since her mate died, but she hadn't ever dared to visit him in his own home before.

Not that she didn't have the right. She could rip his throat out and no one would blame her, Aleksei least of all.

"Hello, Aleksei? Are you home?" Her melodic voice called through the door, being polite since she'd be able to scent that he was inside.

What was she doing here? If she wanted to see him, she could summon him to the pack house. There was definitely something up, that much he could smell. Her emotions were happy and high, which was the last thing he expected of anyone coming to see him these days.

Aleksei pushed his wolf back down and was about to grab his jeans. Wolves had no compunction about being naked in front of each other, since their clothes didn't shift with them, but it somehow felt rude to have his junk hanging out when answering the door.

None of that mattered, because Selena didn't wait to be invited in. She pushed his front door open and came right on in. "Ah, there you are, Aleksei. Going out for a run? I'm glad I caught you."

Aleksei stepped behind the chair. "Uh, yeah. A run."

Selena narrowed her eyes at him, and he knew full well that she had scented his lie and didn't like it. "Good. Running will get whatever has been eating you up out of your system. But it will have to wait, because I have a task for you."

Whatever has been eating him up? Like the fact that her entire life was upended because of him? He'd rarely been scared a day in his life, but he was damn nervous now about what kind of task she wanted him to do. She shouldn't be trusting him to get her groceries, much less do anything important.

"I'm not sure how I can help you, Matriarch." Goddess, he sounded like a wimp.

"That's okay, because I do. Now, go take a shower and put this on while I tidy up a bit in here. We're expected in an hour, so no dilly-dallying." She handed over a garment bag folded over her arm.

So many questions, and he didn't have the gumption to ask a single one. Aleksei reached for the bag, doing his best to keep his lower half hidden behind the furniture. He grabbed the bag and backed out of the living room so as not to further expose himself to the powerful wolftress who was already running her finger along the dust on his furniture.

"You really don't have to clean up. If I'd known you were coming, I could have—"

"Shoo. It's not like I haven't cleaned up after messy boys my whole life. I'll have this place spic and span before you're even done manscaping." She waved him off and headed toward his kitchen.

"Yes, ma'am." Awkward. Even his own mother didn't clean up after him and no one had ever told him to manscape. Aleksei took the hottest and fastest shower of his life, although he did in fact take an extra minute to trim up.

It was getting a bit wrangly down there. Not that he intended any women to get close enough to notice.

Freshly clean, he did feel a bit lighter. Now for whatever was in that garment bag.

Oh fuck.

This was some high-end shit. He'd half expected to see a suit. But what he got was a fresh pair of jeans that probably cost more than his house, a black silk t-shirt, and a jacket that he couldn't afford in a hundred lifetimes.

There was even underwear, socks, and a pair of leather boots that he never would have chosen for himself, but he had to admit they were pretty damn nice. Somehow, every single thing in the bag fit perfectly, like they'd been tailored to fit his broad shoulders and his big ass feet.

Just how long had Selena been planning on coming over here? This was more than some simple task she was asking him to do if she'd had clothes tailored. Now he was even more nervous. But he would deny the widow of his former alpha nothing, so he got dressed, being careful with each item, and presented himself to her for inspection.

"There's the handsome Troika Enforcer I know. Turn around and let me see how the jacket fits from the back." Selena made a little twirling motion with her fingers.

Aleksei had never modeled an outfit in his life, but he dutifully did as he was told. Selena swiped her hands along his shoulders and gave the bottom hem a tug to straighten his jacket. "Perfect. I do have a good eye. Okay, then. Let's go."

"Are you going to tell me where we're going?" He glanced around the living room and kitchen like there might be some clue, but all he saw was that his dishes had been done and the inch-thick dust on his TV was gone. He hadn't even been in the shower that long. Selena must be in with some house elves to get his place looking so sparkling clean so fast.

"Nope. You don't need to know until we get there." She grabbed him by the elbow and led him out of the cabin and to her Tesla SUV. "I'll drive. That way you can't get away."

Selena giggled and Aleksei blanched. Was this some kind of matriarch mafia thing where she was going to drive him out to the desert and shoot him in the back of the head? He gulped down the tinny taste of self-hatred that made him think he deserved that fate. Selena and the Troikas weren't like that. They'd welcomed him home a hero and had their healer work hard to save his life. She would never execute him. Even if he deserved it.

Tonight, he would take whatever punishment Selena wanted to deal him. "I would never try to escape. I am ever the pack's faithful servant."

Selena gave his cheek a grandmotherly squeeze, although to him she didn't look a day over fifty. "We'll see about that. Get in. We don't want to be late."

Selena drove so fast that Aleksei got squished back into his seat. If he didn't know wolftresses had the fastest reactions of pretty much any species on the planet, he would be scared for his life. But they tore through the quiet streets of Rogue without even seeing any other cars. Where the heck was everyone? It was like a national holiday or something—

Ah, shit on a shingle. Today must be Thanksgiving. Selena was taking him to some kind of family dinner. She was right, he was already planning his escape. He wasn't feeling grateful for much these days and he did not want to sit around eating turkey and spilling mashed potatoes and gravy down his shirt with the people he most admired in the world.

"We're here," Selena sing-songed and pulled up in front of the Naughty Wolf.

Oh god. This was even worse than he thought. She wasn't taking him to a family dinner. She was taking him to the strip club. What was next, she'd hand him a roll of dollar bills and tell him to buy something nice for himself? He couldn't take it. "I don't think—"

"I'm gonna stop you right there. Don't think. Just enjoy." Selena got out of the car and waited on the sidewalk for him.

It took Aleksei three deep steadying breaths before he talked himself into getting out of the car. This was definitely going to be one of the weirdest Thanksgivings he'd ever had. He followed his matriarch through the front door of the club and prepared himself for an assault on his nose of alcohol, sweat, and glitter.

What he got was turkey and giggles. Instead of loud music and strippers dancing on the poles, he found a long table set up in the middle of the room with a full Thanksgiving dinner laid out. Men and women mingled around the table including all three of the Troika boys and their mates. His alpha, Max, gave a dude-head-nod of welcome and a grin that said he knew exactly what Selena had been up to.

"I've got someone I want you to meet, Aleksei." Selena grabbed him by the hand and dragged him toward one end of the table. "I expect you to keep this young woman company this evening. She doesn't have any other family and she needs a strong man in her life to boss around."

14

The hits just kept on coming. "You're setting me up on a blind date for Thanksgiving dinner?"

"Not blind at all. You should go into this with your eyes wide open." Selena raised her eyebrows and tilted her chin to the side, indicating he should look behind him.

He turned and was instantly struck by lightning, Thor's hammer, the hand of Zeus. He couldn't breathe, and every hair on his body stood up on end. His wolf pushed to the surface and Aleksei had to swallow hard to keep from howling.

What was causing this extreme reaction?

He'd like to say it was the golden-brown turkey. Yeah. It was definitely that delicious-looking roast bird. It couldn't possibly be the woman carrying the main course toward the table on a platter. No, no. He wasn't affected at all by those plump thighs and juicy breasts.

Gulp. Aleksei found himself licking his lips.

HOLIDATE

*H*oly crap on a cracker. That was the guy that Selena was setting her up with? That guy? With all the muscles on top of muscles? Geez. He had to be one of the Troika pack wolf shifters. He was too good-looking not to be.

Duh. Of course he was. Selena was all about getting all of the single men in the pack matched up with mates. A bead of sweat formed on her top lip and she swiped at it. That's what was truly going on here. The matriarch of the wolf pack wanted her to be a mate. This man's mate.

Umm. What? She'd watched all the cray-cray stuff that Heli went through when she became Kosta's mate. She'd gotten psychic visions. Gal had become a freaking werewolf when she got together with Max. Helena was not even ready to get into a relationship with any guy, much less change her whole damn life for him.

Nope. No way. Even if he was the hottest, yummiest guy she'd ever met in her entire life. No.

She would have to implement the gravy down the front of his shirt plan. Helena bit her lip. Her date already had a scowl on his face. With that kind of mad on, she could tell he didn't want to be here anymore than she wanted him to be. When she poured the bowl of turkey-flavored gloop on him, he was either going to explode and eat her face, or thank her for giving him an excuse to escape this setup.

Selena tugged on the guy's sleeve and dragged him toward the table.

Here goes nothing.

Helena grabbed the gravy as if she intended to move it to the other end of the table and turned so she wasn't facing them straight on. That way, when she turned to greet him, she could accidentally on purpose bump into that amazingly broad chest and oops-a-daisy, gravy goo down his front.

She was not imagining licking all the gravy off of his finely-formed pecs. No she was not.

"Helena dear, I have someone who wants to meet you." The crafty matchmaker shoved the wall of growly man in front of her and right up to Helena's side.

She didn't even have time to enact her plan. The hulk of a wolf man was all up in her space and instead of pouring the gravy down the front of him to get rid of him, she hugged it to her chest. "Hi."

"Hello." His eyes flicked from her own, down to her mouth, and kept going.

Dude was already checking out her rack and they hadn't even exchanged names yet. She wanted to be mad, but instead it made her feel desirable. She knew full well she had great boobs, but she wasn't exactly showing them off tonight. She was wearing a plain old v-neck t-shirt and jeans. What would he be staring at if she had on one of her dancing outfits?

A warm sensation spread over her heart and she licked her lips. This must be that mating thing the girls had talked about. Gal, Heli, and Zara all said they felt something visceral and extra special when they were with their wolves. Was this it? A warm gooey feeling across her skin.

One of his eyebrows went up and his gaze continued down, down, down. "You're dripping gravy."

Helena glanced down and the bowl was tipped just enough so that a small but steady stream of gravy was dribbling down her cleavage. Still, she couldn't seem to move to do anything about it.

Hotty Wolfboy, ahem, make that Wolfman, took the bowl from her and swiped one finger over her sternum, catching the drip and cleaning the gravy from her skin. Where he touched her skin a trail of heat burned into her, much hotter and more intense than the spilled side dish.

She held her breath, waiting to see what he would do next. She wasn't disappointed. He brought his finger up to his mouth and sucked every last drop away. "Mmm."

"Well, I can see my work here is finished. Good job, me." Selena backed away and joined her family at the table.

Helena barely noticed, but Wolfman did. He stepped back and blinked a few times. "Sorry. I shouldn't have—"

He grabbed a napkin from the table and handed it to her.

"Thanks." She took the napkin and wiped the remaining stickiness away. "I'm Helena by the way. I guess we're supposed to be dates for each other tonight."

She wasn't entirely sure how she felt about that anymore. She did not not not need to be fixed up on a blind date. She didn't need any dates for that matter, but the dude was delectable, and Selena did have excellent taste in men. This guy was revving all of Helena's engines and then some.

One particular dribble of gravy was creeping its way down, down, down, right in between her boobs. If she didn't get it now, she'd be sitting around at the party with Eau de Turkey Gravy wafting out of her chest all night. Helena stuck a finger into her shirt trying to catch the drip, then realized what she was doing. She glanced up at her fake date and yep, his eyes were fixed right to her chest. Not that she could blame him. She was rooting around in there pretty obviously.

Whatever, guys would be guys. It wasn't like she didn't have them eyeing her actual boobs every day anyway. At least right now they were covered by several layers of clothes and gravy. She didn't mind his lascivious gaze, that she could handle.

Then he licked his lips.

All of a sudden, he was the big bad wolf and Helena was hoping that his tongue was all the better to eat her with, my dear.

"You missed a spot." He reached his hand out and with one callused finger caressed her skin from the hollow of her throat down to the first button on her shirt. When he pulled his finger away, Helena forgot how to breathe for a second.

The smallest bead of gravy clung to the end of his finger and he brought it up to his lips and tasted the tip with that sexy tongue of his. "Mmm. Salty."

Okay. Helena had never specifically thought anyone's

19

tongue was particularly sexy before. Sure, it could be used to do some sexy stuff, especially between one's lips, either pair. But the actual warm, wet muscle? No. Until now. She was going to have dreams about that tongue. Geez. Had it just gotten hot in here?

"Hey, Helena? You gonna bring that gravy over here or what?"

She was kind of leaning toward 'or what'. If she happened to spill a bit more on herself...ack. Stop it. She didn't even know his name yet. So far, he was simply the hottie with the naughty body.

Besides. She was not doing this with him. Whatever this was. She didn't need a date, she didn't need a man. What she needed was some turkey dinner. "Yep, sorry. I was making a bit of a mess. Here you go."

Helena grabbed the gravy bowl back from him, set it on the table, and sat at the only open spot. Ha. So there. That would show him she didn't need company or his finger or his tongue.

A growling sound came from behind her and one of the other girl's dates, who she happened to sit next to, froze with a bite of green bean casserole midway to his mouth.

Her date stood right behind them with his arms crossed. "You're in my seat."

The guy got up out of the seat so fast he almost spilled his food. "Sorry, man. My bad."

Helena saw Selena roll her eyes in Mr. McGrowly's direction and tsk-tsk at him. That didn't stop him from sitting his ass down in the now-vacant place. He freaking barely fit on the chair. He had the widest shoulders that a girl could so easily wrap herself up in and feel all protected and safe.

What? No. That thought did not come from the deepest darkest parts of her brain. Get the heck out of here with that idea. She was perfectly fine without wolfman hugs.

She slid her gaze over, hoping he wouldn't notice she was eyeballing him. Of course, he was looking right back at her and had a serious mad on. "Don't look at me like that."

His face went from cranky to surprised. Dude clearly wasn't used to a woman calling him out on his shit. But then he did something that gave her butterflies way down deep in her belly.

He smiled.

Holy furballs. That little grin with a hint of wicked lit up his whole damn face and made his eyes twinkle. Damn it. She was such a sucker for twinkling eyes.

"My apologies. I will try not to look at you like that again. But no promises." He winked at her. Actually freaking winked. "I am Aleksei and I have a proposition for you."

"You do, huh? I don't think I like the sound of that." But she did. Ack. No. No, she didn't. What the heck was wrong with her?

"Yes. A very private proposition. How about we go grab another bottle of wine for the group?" He jerked his head toward the bar. "Maybe some champagne to celebrate the holiday?"

Every single word out of Aleksei's mouth dripped with sex. He hadn't even slipped in any innuendos or anything. It was just the way his voice was, all husky and lazy, like he'd just gotten out of bed, or had the most amazing orgasm.

He could read the back of a cereal box to her and she'd happily just hand over her panties. She very clearly already needed a new pair since hers were more than a little damp. "Yeah. Champagne sounds good."

She stood and half-stumbled over her chair. Aleksei caught her by the elbow so she didn't topple over and that completely non-sexual touch zinged through her. A breathy whimper escaped her lips even though she was pretty sure she'd forgotten how to breathe.

He got up from his own seat without his gaze ever veering from her mouth. Good Gods. Was he this tall a minute ago?

"Yes, Helena," he said a bit too loudly. "I will help you get that bottle of champagne, of course. Show me where it is."

Okay. That was awkward and obvious. No, not at all. Whatever. The whole lot of her friends had been pushing her to get some action. If it was clear she and this hunka-hunka were instantly hot for each other, they'd probably all cheer her on if it appeared she was going to get it on in the bar storage room.

"Yeah. I don't think I can reach the bottles on the top shelf all by myself." Helena glanced at the table, but without actually looking at a single person. "Be back in a minute."

"Take your time, dear," Selena said in a too-knowing tone.

"I'd let him pop my cork," one of the girls whispered.

Geez. The sooner she heard Aleksei's proposition, the better. At this point, if the two of them didn't come back all hot and bothered, they'd probably get booed out of the rest of dinner. Helena led him well past the place they actually kept the alcohol and into the back bar.

"What's up?" She was doing her best to act casual in case this wasn't a sexy-times proposal. She leaned against the wall, propped one foot up, and folded her arms.

Aleksei's gaze zeroed in on her foot and followed the line of her leg up, up, up, dragging his wolfy stare across every inch of her body like he was going to eat her up. Helena would not be opposed to that plan.

Maybe she should suggest a no strings attached fling. Or even better, no strings attached sex, but make it look to everyone else that they were heading into serious relationship territory. That would get Selena and the girls off her back. Aleksei would probably go for it, right? He was a dude, of course he would.

Now, let's see. How to suggest it to him without sounding eager? She should be very casual about it so as not to scare him off and make him think she wanted anything more.

He was already fucking her with his eyes. Yummy. Probably it would be easiest just to blurt out her idea and see how he reacted. Helena put on her best come hither bedroom eyes, licked her lips, and was just about to ask him. She didn't get the chance.

Aleksei growled dark and deep in his chest, she could feel it. He moved so fast she barely registered it until he was right up into her personal space bubble. His arms wrapped around her waist, and pulled her flush to him. He lowered his face and brushed his lips across hers so lightly she wasn't even sure if it was his skin or the electricity between them. Either way, her body was fritzing all over the place.

"*Lisichka*, keep looking at me exactly like that as I ask you this question."

Yeah. No problem. It didn't matter what the question was. With their bodies pressed together like this she couldn't stop looking at him like the tastiest piece of pie on the planet, even if she wanted to.

"Good. Just like that. Looks like we've both got a room full of people pushing us toward each other. I'd sure as hell like to get a certain matchmaker off my back. If you and I pretend to hook up, we'll both be free to live our lives however the fuck we want. You game?"

What was that saying about sex-addled brains thinking alike? Great minds, it was great minds and they were completely on the same wave length. This clench was just for show. Perfect. That's what she wanted. Totally. One hundred percent.

"I'm down to play." As long as he didn't play with her heart. He wouldn't. She had the uncomfortable feeling she was the one using her emotions like a toy.

"Then let's show the peanut gallery back there we're both planning to score." His eyes went fifty shades darker and that electricity zinging between their lips crashed like a thousand bolts of lightning as he finally closed the last millimeter and kissed her.

His lips were soft, which sent her senses going haywire because this kiss was nothing even close to gentle. His tongue thrust inside. He stole the breath from her and didn't give it back. This rough way he took her mouth, like he was claiming it for himself, had all of her long-ignored desires popping their heads up and cheering.

She should break the kiss. Say something funny and break this tension between them. All the ideas of funny sports references she could come up with flew straight out of her head and were quickly replaced with visions of that tongue of his doing the same taking and tasting and thrusting all over her body.

If this was a hello kiss, she was going to be in a lot of trouble when it came time for the goodbye.

UNBROKEN

*H*elena was so hot in Aleksei's arms. If he didn't burn up in a fireball of lust, he was going to melt into a puddle of sexual need and desire on the floor right in front of her. The moment her lips hit his he knew. God dammit. He. Knew.

She was his fated mate, the one woman in the world made especially for him. His body stood up and cheered, his heart was already sending out the mating ceremony invitations, but his brain was pulling the emergency brake.

He never should have suggested a fake relationship. If he didn't put a stop to it right away, he wouldn't be able to help himself. He'd mark her and claim her for his own. That was something he couldn't do. He would not condemn this beautiful, vibrant woman to a living hell of being the mate of a nothing such as he'd become.

Except she felt so good in his arms, so perfect, so fucking...his.

Helena's tongue danced with his, daring him to play her sexy games. Despite his mind telling him this was all kinds of wrong, he couldn't help reveling in the kiss. Just one. He'd savor her smoking hot mouth and keep that memory close for all eternity. This brief moment in time would ease his suffering night after night as he remembered how absolutely right they were for each other.

Aleksei pushed his hands into her hair, gripping the strands tight and holding her to him so he could taste every bit of those sexy little whimpers she made. Her hand went to his ass and gave it a squeeze.

Fuck, how he loved a confident, eager woman. He returned the favor, sending one hand wandering up and down her back, caressing the curve at her waist, and tracing down over her hip. His cock was straining against his jeans and nothing but her body would give him the relief he needed.

Okay, so he was going to savor this kiss and a bit more. No harm in a little dry humping. Aleksei walked the two of them back, never once letting their lips part. He put one hand over her head on the slats of wood and used his own body to press her against the wall. Bottles of liquor rattled and the next second the turkey-eaters were catcalling and whistling at them from the other room.

Helena didn't seem to care because she didn't break the kiss either. This could all be an act from her. She'd agreed to pretending to hook up as fast as he suggested it. She was probably putting on a show for her friends. She already had the skills to make people believe she was all about sex and emotion. In her job, that came with the territory.

Exotic dancers had great acting skills. He was sure of that. There was no way he could tell if any of her pure heat was real. She sure tasted and felt like she wasn't faking a thing. He shouldn't be worrying about, anyway.

He was the one who wanted, no needed, this budding relationship to be pretend. They were putting on a show, he had to play his part too. Fine. Good. He could do that.

Aleksei broke the kiss and nipped at her lip one last time. A little too loud, he said, "I always wanted to fuck a stripper."

Helena's jaw dropped and her eyes shot daggers at him. Yeah. He was that asshole.

If she was really his true soul mate...and she was, he knew that deep in his heart...Aleksei had to do everything in his power to protect her. Protect her from himself and his long list of sins. He was no good for her. He wasn't even any good as an enforcer for his own pack.

He could simply add unrequited love to his mountains of bullshit. Helena didn't need to get roped into a wolf shifter relationship. Not with someone like him.

Under her breath, Helena whispered, "You want to make this fake relationship work, you'd better pull your head out of your asshole. Don't think you can ever disrespect me or my profession again. You got me?"

Before he could even sheepishly nod, she reached her arm back and came at him. He deserved to be slapped in the face for being a giant dick. What he got was a sharp couple of pokes in the chest. Like his heart didn't already hurt.

She moved her head slightly to the side and raised her voice as loud as he had. "Baby, you know I got the goods. So if you want some of my sugar, sweeten your ass up. Otherwise you can get in line and take a number."

Even his bulk and wolf abilities were no match for her badass girl power. Fuck, that was sexy as hell. "I want all your sugar, mama. I won't promise to behave, but I will look forward to you trying to make me."

Fiery spirit flashed in Helena's eyes. Oh, so she liked being challenged, did she? He'd have to remember that. She moved like she was going to pull away from him and go back to the party. He couldn't have that. If this fake relationship plan was going to work and get everyone off their backs, they needed to sell it, right here, right now.

"Let's get out of here and see just how much fun we can have while you try to tame me." Aleksei pulled Helena back to him, laid one more hot, quick kiss on her, and grabbed her hand. He took a step toward the door and gave her a tug, but not too hard. She needed to know he wasn't trying to force her to do anything.

"Come with me. Let our fan club think all kinds of dirty-minded things about where we're going and what we're about to do. Once we're out those doors, I can go home, and you can do whatever it was you wanted to do today instead of getting set up on a blind date with me." He purposefully let his shoulders drop and his muscles relax so he appeared nonchalant about this deal he was making with the devil.

"Fine," she whispered back. "But only because I don't want to get set up anymore. I actually did want to hang out with my friends today and eat more turkey than is reasonable."

"I'm sure some do-gooder will bring me leftovers. I promise, you can have them all." He gave her a little wink and another tug toward the door. With one last look back toward the happy party, she followed him out the back door of the Naughty Wolf. The sooner he could get out of here the better.

Geez, he was an asshole. Selena and the Troikas were only trying to do right by him. He was the one being a bastard, taking Helena away from her friends so he could go home – and what? Mope. Hide away in the comforting dark of his cabin and avoid real life.

He had even more to brood about now that he'd found Helena. What fucking shitty timing to find his mate at this point in his life. Man, he hoped she didn't feel the pull of that bond the same way he did. He wanted her to be happy and healthy, which was not something she could do with him. He would never tie her to him in that way. Never.

The least he could do was make sure she was taken care of.

Even if she found love with another, a human, he would still need to take care of her. The thought of her being with anyone else, shit, even looking at another man, gave him a punch right in the gut. His stomach literally physically hurt. This was going to be a hell of a lot harder than he thought.

Once they were out into the early evening air, he dropped her hand, and yet again felt like an ass. No wolf should treat his mate the way he was treating Helena. Better that both she and his damn wolf learned now that there would be no mating.

"Crap. My keys are in the office. Will it look too weird if I pop back in there to get them?" She glanced back at the door.

"No. You gotta have your keys and stuff. But let's make it look good. Come here." Aleksei held his hand out to her, even though he shouldn't ever freaking touch her again.

She took it before he could change his mind. In a blink she was back in his arms and he was kissing her again. One hand went into her hair and the other straight to her luscious ass.

Dear Goddess in the sky, he should not be touching her soft, sweet curves, but he couldn't help it. Especially not when she was melting in his arms, and her tongue was in his mouth. He hiked her skirt up on one side and scraped his fingers over her bare flesh. He was dying to know what kind of lacy, slinky underthings she had on. Or didn't.

Helena broke the kiss with a soft whimper. "If these are your fake kisses, I can't imagine what your real ones are like. Some girl is going to be very, very lucky to land you one day."

She took a deep breath and then stepped away. Her hair was a mess from his fingers running through it, and she looked thoroughly well kissed, on her way to being well fucked. She yanked her skirt a little higher and opened the door.

Right. Get her keys.

"I'll be right back." She walked, a little wobbly, into the club and Aleksei grabbed the door to hold it open simply so he could watch that ass wiggle back and forth with each of her steps.

Fuck. He needed to stop drooling. He also needed to tell his cock to cool it. No action besides his hand would be had tonight. And that's how he wanted it. Dammit.

Deep breaths, and thoughts of baseball, the Queen of England, and coronavirus, and the trouble in his pants went back to its usual non-desperate state. Good. It needed to stay that way. It would probably help if he would quit kissing Helena.

31

Kissing her lips, kissing her neck, then sinking down to his knees and kissing her—

"Okay, I'm ready, we can each go home or whatever now." Helena dangled her keys in his face.

Well, fuck. There went his cock right back up to half mast again. He cleared his throat and shifted his weight, trying hard to adjust his pants without looking like that's what he was doing. "Great. I'll walk you home."

She frowned at him and damn, if her pout wasn't just as enticing as her smile. Shit, shit, shit. He had to stop thinking about her lips.

"You don't have to do that. I just live a few blocks—"

A deep growl built up in his chest and rumbled right out of his mouth before he could even tell his beast to cool its jets. "No. You will not walk alone at night."

Helena blinked at him like he had a wolf growing out of his head. She raised one finger and looked like she was about to tell him off. Again.

Wait. He didn't, did he? Had that seriously just happened? Aleksei hadn't lost control of his shift since puberty, for Goddess' sake. He patted his head and ran his finger through his hair. "Sorry. I didn't mean it to come out like I was some controlling asshole. I have no right to tell you what to do. It would make me feel better if you'd let me walk you home."

Helena's finger didn't go down and if those narrowed eyes were any indication, she was pissed. "It's a damn good thing you caught yourself there, buster. Because A. Nobody tells me what to do. And B. I do what I want. You remember that and we'll get along just fine."

Goddess, a woman who didn't take shit from anyone was

hot. Aleksei folded his arms and grinned at her. He could not help wondering if she'd let him tell her what to do if they were in his bed and he had her arms pinned over her head and his other hand between her legs. "Won't happen again."

Tonight.

"Good. Then yes, walk me home. If anyone sneaks a peek they'll think we're going to my place to get it on." She turned on her heel and headed down the sidewalk.

Aleksei followed after her like a puppy on a string. A puppy who was on high alert and examining every shadow for potential threats. Helena might know about his world, but no human outside of the ones who'd mated the wolves in the Troika pack knew the extent of the war.

Niko had ended most of the infighting when he became the Wolf Tzar. But there were still a few one-blood bastards out there that would love to take out a Troika Enforcer, or his mate. Just the thought of a one-blood getting anywhere near Helena had his wolf rising back up to the surface.

Mark her.

Claim her.

Mate her.

Grr.

Aleksei hurried to catch up to Helena and took her hand in his. "Just in case someone is watching us."

That same zing went from her skin to his and he squeezed her hand tighter. Helena tipped her head to the side and the slyest of smiles turned the corner of her lips up at the edges. All that anger at him melted away and the sizzle between them was back.

Too bad he had to let that sizzle fizzle. Just a minute

more. He knew he had to let her go, but she felt so damn good and he wasn't used to anything that made him feel...anything. He'd take it while he could.

Theirs wasn't a leisurely stroll up the walk. Even if this was a fake rendezvous, they were making it look like they were in a hurry to get to a bedroom. Was Helena doing that on purpose, was she that eager to get rid of him? Or could it be that she was genuinely anxious to take him home and into her bed?

They did have some serious chemistry between them. He knew why. She likely didn't. Humans didn't know about fated mates until they were pulled into the wolf world, like the Troika alphas' women had been.

Aleksei knew all about how human women thought. Helena wasn't the first one he'd been interested in. At the beginning of the pack wars he'd been getting down and dirty with a hot piece of human ass. But that's all she'd been to him. He'd never shared his true self with her, hadn't confided in her that he was a wolf-shifter.

Once he'd come back from the Crescent pack a broken man, that relationship had gone down the tubes real fast. If he couldn't tell her he was a wolf enforcer, he certainly couldn't turn to her in his darkest moments and admit that he'd been forced to watch silently as his alpha was politely poisoned.

Aleksei's stomach churned. He was one weak-ass enforcer who hadn't even been able to see through the treachery of a wolftress even as she tempted him with the same wolfsbane that killed Piotr Troika.

He wasn't fit to be with a human, he wasn't fit to be with a wolf. He surely wasn't fit to be with his one true mate.

The sun was setting now, and Helena's skin, hair, and eyes shimmered in the dusky evening. The moon wasn't yet full, but shone bright on the horizon. She was so fucking beautiful and that scared the living shit out of Aleksei. He was a fool for thinking he could be anywhere near her and not ruin her life like he had destroyed his own.

Helena turned her key in the lock and smiled over at him. "Do you want to—"

"I gotta go. I'll, uh, call you." He bolted off her front step and into the nearest alleyway. His wolf howled in his mind, chastising him for leaving his mate alone and unprotected.

The second he was out of sight he let the wolf take over and his bones cracked, his muscles reshaped themselves, and his skin split as his fur burst out of him, busting right through the fancy clothes Selena had insisted he wear. His paws hit the dirty concrete and immediately turned back toward Helena's place.

It took all Aleksei's will to overpower that innate instinct. It took truly admitting to himself, he would upend her life by claiming her. That was what it took to make his wolf realize that even being anywhere near her was putting her in danger.

Aleksei took off in a fast run toward the Reserve where he could run and run and run until he was so exhausted he couldn't return to Helena even if he wanted to.

PIE VS SEXY TIMES

ell, that was a weird fucking day. Helena stared at the back of her door for a full minute before she shrugged, dumped her bag and her keys on the little table just inside, and headed toward the kitchen.

Dammit. She was supposed to have Thanksgiving leftovers to snack on. Pie. She should have at least four flavors of leftover pie. A couple pieces to eat tonight until she was uncomfortably full, as anyone should be on Thanksgiving Day, and another two for breakfast the next couple of days.

Mmm. Pie for breakfast was the best. It was even better as morning after breakfast.

Now, because she'd agreed to have a temporary fake boyfriend, she had neither the sex nor any of the goodies to sustain her during the holiday aftermath. She wasn't a hundred percent sure that trade off was worth it. No, wait. It was if he actually held up his end of the bargain and got her out of all the awkward where's-your-date questions over the next few months.

The holidays were the worst for peer pressure to have a mate.

Mate? That was a strange word. Why had she thought that?

Must be the lack of sugar. Or the lack of sex. Especially after those sweet, hot, delicious kisses Aleksei had laid on her.

Helena popped open her freezer and pulled out a container of whipped cream she'd been saving for her left-overs. This would have to do. The first spoonful was delicious. The second was meh. The third? Downright revolting. This dessert topping needed some dessert, and she didn't mean the edible kind.

Whipped cream was good for all kind of fun things. None of which she had or was going to get, because...fake boyfriend. Ugh.

No boyfriend and no pie. One of those two things she could fix, and she knew the absolute best person to call for help. Heli owed her one anyway.

Helena texted her best friend the pie emoji and the praying hands emoji.

Heli immediately messaged back with the universal sign for no.

No? Heli was being a pie hoarder and Helena knew it. This called for the big guns. She dialed Heli's number. It rang and rang and rang. No answer.

Super not fair. Now it was war. Helena typed out another text and her phone rang almost immediately.

Heli panted like she'd been on a marathon run. "You are not coming over to my house and stealing my pie."

She needed this. Bad. "Yes, I am."

"Get your own pie." The phone muffled at the end of that sentence and there was some sort of a squeal in the background.

"I want yours. It's the best. And you're my best friend so you have to help me in my time of need."

"Fine." She huffed, in that way only a bestie who always had your back did. "You gotta give me at least another, uh, fifteen minutes."

She might die of pie withdrawals in that amount of time. "What? Why?"

There was some sort of a tussle and it sounded like Heli dropped the phone. When she came back on, her voice had gone down about four octaves and had a distinct alpha male growl to it. "Because she's busy getting whipped cream licked off of every inch of her body at the moment."

"Oh. Hi, Kosta. Tell her to call me when you're, uh, finished." Helena remembered the point of her call and shouted into the phone hoping Heli would hear before Kosta hung up. "Bring me pie!"

Man, she hoped that worked because without any pie, she was going to be getting mighty desperate. For food. Yeah. food.

Kosta must have some magical sexy times skills, because Heli was at her door in about fifteen minutes. Helena wasn't jealous at all of her sex-mussed hair or that rosy glow on her cheeks. They made a great couple.

"I come bearing presents," Heli sing-songed and pushed her way in through the little front hallway and straight to the kitchen. "I'll dish up pie while you dish about your insta-connection with hot and growly Aleksei."

Only for homemade desserts made by Heli would she

even consider talking about what had happened between she and...no, wait. She couldn't say anything because there was no relationship. It was fake and Helena didn't want to lie to her best friend.

Oh God, why had she agreed to this dumb plan again? Probably because she was mostly thinking with her hoo-ha and not her head.

"So, when's the wedding?" Heli shoved a piece of pumpkin pie covered in just the right amount of whipped cream into Helena's hands.

Oh, right. That's why. Because everyone and their mothers wanted her to get a fricking boyfriend...or in Heli's case, a husband. "Don't start with me, you smartass. Just because you're blissfully married, doesn't mean I need to be.

"I see. So it's just about the sex." Heli took a bite of her own slice and groaned from the deliciousness.

"We haven't had sex, so no." In fact, she couldn't remember the last time she had sex, it had been that long. As her body was currently reminding her by craving everything naughty under the sun.

Heli's fork paused midway to her mouth. "Wait. What? You're telling me after the way you two left the Friends-giving all over each other, that he chastely walked you home and went on his merry way? I'm not buying that for one teeny-tiny second. Good try, thanks for playing."

Helena was royally screwing this up. Maybe she should just tell Heli what was going on. But what was going on? This whole fake relationship thing, sure, but if that was all, then she shouldn't have this monster attraction to Aleksei. He was hot, she'd give him that, but so was every other guy who came into the club. She didn't go all twitterpated for just anyone.

Her twitters were definitely pated. Helena avoided replying to Heli by scooping a big bite of pie into her mouth. She licked her fork clean and damn if that didn't lead to fantasies of licking Aleksei's, uh...fork.

Heli stared her down. She wasn't going to be able to avoid answering that question. Fine. "Sort of. We maybe made out a little more after we left the party, but he didn't come into my house and he isn't here now."

None of that was a lie. So far so good.

"Uh-oh." Heli's eyes went wide. "He left you all hot and alone? He did. That asshat. That's why the desperate cry for pie. Or is there something you're not telling me?"

Heli pointed her fork right at Helena's face. How was she going to get out of this? Tried and true, she would answer a question with a question. "Is there something you aren't telling me?"

That shouldn't have worked, but Heli looked away. That sneak. "Heli. Is there something I should know about Aleksei? I know he's part of the Troikas pack and so that makes him a wolf-shifter. I've never dated one. Not that I'd know if I had. Dish, girl."

"You two haven't...no. That's silly. It's not the full moon."

Helena didn't know all the ins and outs of wolf-shifter culture, but she didn't think that whole full-moon turn into a werewolf thing was a part of it. "What does that have to do with anything? Something particular happens then? Because if you say he's gonna go all crazy and try to eat me during the full moon, I don't think I will believe you."

"Nothing. Yet. Just...how do you actually feel around

40

Aleksei? Is it like just sexy times attraction or...?" Heli looked down at Helena's chest.

Umm. Wait. Not her chest. Her neck. Helena reached up and rubbed the spot Aleksei had scraped his teeth across. She didn't think he'd left her a hickey or anything.

Helena did not like talking about feelings. Feelings were for suckers. "He's totally hot and a great kisser. I'm sure we will be great in bed when we get there. He's probably just playing the anticipation card."

"Yeah. Maybe. But wolf-shifters aren't usually like that. Not once they've..." Heli cut herself off from finishing her sentence with another bite of pie.

"Don't make me steal the rest of your pie. Stop holding back from whatever it is you want to say." Helena pointed her fork at her friend like a weapon. Not as good as Wonder Woman's lasso of truth, though. The Pie Fork of Truth didn't quite have the same ring to it. "If I can't find out from you, then I'll go ask someone else, you poop."

"Okay. But don't freak out." Heli waited to continue until Helena put her fork back in her pie and nodded her agreement. "Once a wolf-shifter finds his mate, he doesn't hold back."

Mate?

Like fated mate? One true mate? The. One?

No way, nuh-uh.

Wolves were crazy for believing in crap like fate. "I'm clearly not his mate or whatever, because he's not here."

Aleksei had definitely held himself back. Except when he hadn't. Like when they had their tongues in each other's mouths ready to rip their clothes off. "How does the mate, I mean the woman, feel?"

Heli waggled her eyebrows at her. "Like she can't wait to rip his clothes off."

Uh-oh. "Wait. Who wouldn't want to rip the clothes off any superhot guy like Aleksei? That's just a normal response."

"Umm. Like Aleksei, or him specifically?"

She didn't want to answer that question. She wanted the answer to be that any guy would get her all hot and bothered. But the truth was, no guy had revved her up in months. Maybe longer. "Does it matter?"

"Yes." Heli took the last bite of pie, set her plate aside, and leaned in. "Tell me this. When you touch him does it feel like electricity laced with a conga beat going on in your pants? That deep down beyond your heart and into your soul that you need to be with him?"

"Come on, that's just sexual attraction. I'm not denying the guy is hot and that I wouldn't kick him out of my bed." She definitely wished he was in her room sprawled across her bed waiting for her right now. Helena squeezed her legs together to keep the excitement going on down there contained.

"Mmm-hmm, and once you got him there, could you kick him out even if you wanted to?"

Of course she could. Probably. Most definitely. Maybe? She had a joke about it all depending on what he did to her in there, but it somehow got stuck in her throat. She wanted Aleksei in her bed and in her life.

Damn it.

No she didn't. No way, no how. She did not need a man, except to fool all her friends into thinking she had a serious relationship so they wouldn't bug her at all the upcoming holidays.

"Yes. Yes, I could." The only thing keeping Helena's pants from erupting into liar, liar fire was the waterfall between her legs just thinking about Aleksei.

Heli didn't have to say her 'whatever' out loud. The smirk said it for her, loud and clear. She didn't believe Helena's answer even a smidgen. "You keep telling yourself that, my friend. I don't know if you two are fated mates or not, that's not my special ability. If you really want to know, go ask Selena. I do know Aleksei is a little broken and grumpy, but he's a Troika and that makes him a great guy. You could do worse."

Helena had done worse. Too many times. She'd never had the best taste in men. It was simply too hard for her to believe there was a good guy out there for her.

Heli had found one, though. "Did you really feel all that for Kosta when you met him? Not just having the hots for him, but that heart and soul stuff."

Helena hadn't ever felt those mushy gooshy feelings for anyone. She wasn't even sure she knew what they were. More importantly, she'd decided she didn't want love anyway. It was a nuisance. It only let to heartache.

Instead of worrying about falling for Aleksei, she should just hop on that hot body and enjoy the ride, heck, the whole damn rodeo. He was the one who suggested a no strings attached fake relationship. If they were agreed on that, why not throw sex into the equation? Couldn't hurt. In fact, it would feel good. Really good.

Besides, if he was really her fated mate, he wouldn't have asked for this secret sham situation. Fine. Good. That was simply proof that they weren't destined to be together forever.

Helena tried to breathe a sigh of relief. That backfired on her and gave her indigestion instead. Ow. No more pie.

"I feel all that and so much more for Kosta. It took me a while to admit it though."

"Yeah, well you are bull-headed. Unlike me." Ha. That was a lie straight from the pits of hell. "I imagine Kosta had to wine you and dine you to win you over, didn't he?"

"Nope. You'll see. Or maybe you won't. I don't know. But my very friendly advice is that you keep your heart open and see where it leads you."

Heart schmart. Helena was a wise woman and had learned not to rely on her heart for anything. She didn't need it to tell her Aleksei was hot and she wanted more from him. Her head was the part that reminded her more didn't have to mean marriage and commitment. This pretend relationship could be just what she needed.

HIS ONE WEAKNESS

*A*leksei slammed his front door shut, splintering the wood around the frame. His little cabin felt too small, like the walls were closing in on him. He turned right back around and shoved the door open again.

The cool night air did nothing to calm his frazzled anger. He was the ultimate dumbass. His wolf thought so too. He'd left his mate wet and wanting all the way on the other side of town.

Dumb.

Ass.

The second he realized Helena was the one, he should have walked right the hell out of that club and never looked back. Instead, he'd practically dry-humped her against the wall and kissed her.

Kisses that would be burned on his brain for all eternity. So sweet, yet so hot and sexy all at the same time.

What he needed was a good long hard run to work off this frustration and tension. He could beat himself up for miles and miles, hopefully get himself so exhausted he could fall into a deep sleep and not dream of her and all those luscious, mind-blowing, fill-his-hands-up curves.

He threw the shredded clothes he'd grabbed after shifting and tossed them onto the old rocker on the front porch. The scent of her, like pumpkin spice lattes with a shot of dark Kentucky bourbon, wafted through the air from his clothes. They smelled of her.

He wanted badly, so very badly, to go pick his shirt back up, hold it up to his nose, and breathe her in. His wolf was already itching to shift and run back toward his mate. Not gonna happen. Aleksei controlled his shift a few minutes longer and took off, jogging into the woods in the opposite direction of Helena's house.

A few hundred yards in, he let the shift take over. Aleksei reveled in the pain of his bones and skin breaking to shift. The discomfort never even bothered him before. He'd shifted thousands of times in his years, but tonight he wanted the aches to distract both him and his wolf from that driving need to go to her.

There were plenty of places he could run to tonight to torture himself. The area far to the north in what used to be the Crescent pack's territory where he and Piotr had been captured, for one. Or worse, the pit where his alpha had been slaughtered and his own life spared.

Those memories would easily overpower his thoughts of Helena. She was all that was good and right in the world. Everything Aleksei didn't deserve.

For the way he'd let his pack down, he deserved a lonely existence. He should never be allowed to love anyone. He'd only disappoint them if he did. The rest of his life should be a punishment for his crimes. If Max or Niko wouldn't make him pay for letting the Crescent bastards murder their father right in front of his eyes, he was honor bound to show them exactly how contrite and miserable a wolf he truly was.

Every day they allowed him to live, he must sacrifice his own happiness.

But what about Helena?

Aleksei's wolf didn't like this dark mental path they were on. The bond between fated mates linked them irrevocably, forever. If he never marked and claimed her, she might be able to find some dumb human to spend her life with. She could create the life she deserved with a husband or lover.

The wolf jerked their run to a sudden stop and howled mournfully at the moonless sky.

If Helena even so much as looked at another man, Aleksei might have to kill any dudes who caught her eye. Which was not a nice thing to do. Helena would be pretty damn mad if he went around murdering all her beaux.

He couldn't live seeing her with anyone else, though. Which meant only one thing. He was going to have to leave Rogue and never come back. Might as well start now. He'd head north. There were plenty of wide-open spaces to run and keep far, far from humanity in the wilds of Canada.

Good. That was the plan then.

Except he couldn't get his wolf to move. The beast inside was having nothing to do with this idea. He sat down on his haunches and hung out his tongue, panting and whining. Aleksei wasn't even sure if he shifted back into human form if he would be able to break free from his inner wolf's demand.

That was a new one. He'd never pissed his wolf off so bad

47

that it took over. Aleksei stretched and turned and shook, but the wolf would not move his ass. Great. So, what, he was just going to sit in the Reserve forever? Because he was not going back to Rogue to destroy Helena's life.

That's when he smelled it.

At first the breeze had just the hint of an earthy scent that didn't belong. Like a pine tree, but one that wasn't from around here, or a bug not native to New York. Underneath that dissonant smell was much more than simply flora or fauna out of place. There was something cold about it, like ice or permafrost.

There was also the unmistakable scent of a wolf shifter male. A lone wolf.

Aleksei's own wolf chastised him for being such a nincompoop. He wasn't just pouting, the beast had known something was wrong, the over-thinking, morose, broody human part of him had been too distracted to notice.

Nose to the ground, head back in the game, Aleksei searched for the source of the mysterious lone wolf's scent. It wasn't very strong, so it couldn't have been through this part of the Reserve recently.

Why had it been here at all? Was this a one-blood come to sow discontent in the heart of Tzar Nikolaus Troika's reign? It could be a scout, not a lone wolf at all, sent to reconnoiter and find the Troikas' weaknesses. That couldn't happen, wouldn't happen, if Aleksei had anything to say about it.

Except he was one of the Troikas' weaknesses.

The weakest link in the pack's chain. He wasn't even a Troika Enforcer anymore. The enforcer team probably already knew about this threat and his report wouldn't be help or harm. He couldn't take that chance. Regardless if this was a lone wolf or someone allied with the pain in the ass one-bloods, it was a threat.

A threat that could harm his mate.

His wolf was ready to revolt and never let him shift back into human form if he didn't take immediate action to protect his mate. On this one thing the wolf would always win. No matter how much of a shit Aleksei felt like, he would do whatever he could to protect Helena.

Even if he couldn't protect her from himself.

Aleksei followed the scent of the lone wolf on a convoluted path through the Reserve. Either this wolf was drunk, or he had no idea where he was going. He'd been up and down and round and round, but he wasn't going anywhere in particular.

The only place the scent became stronger to indicate that the lone wolf had spent more time there was in the sacred clearing where the Troika pack had their mating rituals. Still there was no sign of this stranger other than the tell-tale way he'd scouted every inch of the Reserve. It was as if he'd circled the area multiple times to learn every tree, rock, and hiding spot.

If he was still in these woods, Aleksei would sniff him out and bring him to Max. Unless of course he put up a fight. Then Aleksei would be more than happy to take the frustrations of the day out on him.

The trail picked up again near the little path that humans used to hike through the woods. It led from one populated part of town to another. This lone wolf was headed right for the old town district. Aleksei picked up his pace and pounded the dirt until he hit the edge of the parking lot.

The lone wolf hadn't stopped there. Any human up late at night might have seen him and made a lot of trouble for the Troikas. Sure, there were some humans who knew about the supernatural now, but only those who were mated to one. Even his ex was now mated and happy.

Max, Kosta, and Niko had started a revolution allowing wolf shifters to find their true mates, one that the Troika pack had happily embraced. But it didn't mean shifters could just wander around town in their beast form. The humans weren't quite ready yet to make friends with fairy tales.

If Max found out, he was going to eat this interloper's face off. If Niko found out, the wolf would wish he'd never been born. Aleksei would like to be the one who brought this dumbass to justice.

He checked carefully to make sure no humans were about, because he wasn't going to shift into human form to keep following the trail. He couldn't. He'd left his clothes back at his cabin. He hadn't expected to go on a wild goose chase, or rather wild wolf chase.

As soon as he was sure he wouldn't be spotted, Aleksei darted across the road and into the alley behind the strip of businesses. Oh, yeah. The wolf's scent was strong here, fresh. He'd been here recently.

The lone wolf wasn't just passing through, either. As Aleksei followed his nose it was clear that the wolf was very interested in Troika-run businesses. Just like in the woods, the scent was all over the building where the pie shop and the Sleepy Folk speakeasy did business. It was a good thing everything in town closed down at two in the morning because it sure as shit looked like the lone wolf had tried to find a way into the bar.

If he'd been here, where else had the intruder been?

Aleksei's heart skipped a half dozen beats. This alley started behind Sleepy Folk, but it ended at the back door of The Naughty Wolf. Where Helena worked.

He sprinted up the alley at top speed. What if she was there? She could have gone back to clean up and close up after the Friendsgiving party. His wolf went mad with rage and worry that his mate could be in harm's way. The lone wolf was dead if he even thought about harming Aleksei's woman.

As much as he didn't want to admit she was his mate and he was hers, they were fated mates and she was his woman. He wouldn't slink away into that dark night and leave her unprotected. He may be a failure as a wolf pack enforcer and a douchecanoe of a lover, but he would not allow Helena to be harmed. Ever.

Aleksei followed his nose all the way around the outside of the building. The outsider had definitely been here, and same as in the rest of the town, not just passing by. He was scoping the place out. He'd spent a lot of time sniffing around each of the doors as if looking for a way in. There didn't appear to be any scent on the door handles. If he was a shifter, why hadn't he changed forms and tried to get in the old-fashioned way, by using the doorknob?

This lone wolf had clearly been here recently. He should be able to track it down and take it out. But that wasn't his job anymore. He wasn't an enforcer. His job now was only to keep Helena safe from the threat. His wolf pulled at him to return to her side. It wanted a whole lot more than to simply protect her.

Aleksei followed the scent trail to the end of the alleyway

and almost got himself run over. The Bay County trash truck was loud and stinky and couldn't be missed. His head was not in the game. He shouldn't even be in town in his wolf form, and now it was already dawn. Damn.

It seemed like the trail of the lone wolf headed out of town, not anywhere near Helena's place, but with the garbage truck leaking sludge all over the street and alley, the scent was lost and he couldn't be positive. He needed to skedaddle and report this problem to his pack alpha.

If the sanitation services were already out and about, he'd better get a move on before he was caught in town in his shifter form. He took off down the deserted space between the buildings and toward the Troika pack house. Hopefully Max and Kosta would both be there so he could eat two birds in one bite.

Kosta would definitely want to know that a lone wolf was sniffing around his business and his employees. Hopefully they'd send a whole pack of Troika Enforcers on the case. At least two for each of the women who worked there. They needed to be protected.

Aleksei's wolf snarled in his head. No one would be protecting Helena but him.

SCHMOES AND UH-OHS

*H*elena promised Kosta that Black Friday would make back all the money he had lost by closing for Thanksgiving. They had dollar drafts, cheap well drink specials, and some of the girls even offered to do two for one on lap dances. Get the gentlemen who frequented the club to bring their friends, and tonight everyone would make a killing.

But with cheap liquor you got cheap schmoes who got handsy. So Kosta had agreed to up the security and have a couple of his more growly guys bouncing tonight to keep the girls safe and happy. Helena had worked at plenty of clubs in her time that didn't care a hoot for what went on, so long as they made money. Now that she was in charge, Helena didn't plan to run the club that way. She wanted to keep both the employees and the owners happy.

She didn't care who Kosta sent to work the door, as long as they had muscles and a scowl. What she didn't expect was to see Aleksei come walking in wearing a black Naughty

Wolf Security t-shirt that was a little too tight. This man really did have muscles on top of muscles.

Yum.

She was in so much trouble with this guy. She should not be drooling all over herself from top to down below. He'd left her high and not so dry last night without any leftovers to her name, not even pie. Mad is what she should be at him. Instead she was getting all hot and bothered.

No. Bad Helena. Stop it, right now.

She did not lose her head over a hot guy even if he was more delicious than hot apple pie. Gah. What was it about this guy that had her going dumb in the head?

At the club was not the place to lose herself over a guy. Even if he was the best damn kisser who ever kissed. Ever. Ack. She was going to have one hell of a hard time concentrating with Hotty McHotsalot around. Making eyes and drooling over him did not pay her rent. Lap dances did. Just because she was managing the place now, it didn't mean that she wasn't dancing as well.

Yeah. That's right, she needed to keep her head in the game, because it was going to be a busy night and she could make her whole month's normal income just in tips on a good Black Friday. She simply needed to get that first lap dance going to get her mojo on. A quick scan of the room showed she was already off her game. Every single one of the other girls had a guy or two or more panting for her and shoving money where they couldn't get it back.

All except Becca. Who was heading straight for Aleksei. What. The. Hell?

Everyone knew the bouncers were off limits during open

hours. What they did in their spare time, or who they did in this case, was no concern of Helena's. But no one was doing Aleksei, except her. She had a relationship with him, dammit. A fake one, but no one else knew that.

Helena marched across the room, her six-inch clear lucite stripper heels clacking with each step she took, as if she was marking her territory.

Becca still beat her to the door where Aleksei was stationed. She batted her eyelashes at him and lifted up her leg, caressing the back of his calf with her heel as she ran her fingers down his arm. She even arched her back so her girls were on display and giggled while twirling her hair. All moves Helena herself had taught her. Helena was going to murder her with her own heels.

"Ooh, Aleksei, that is such a sexy name. How come we haven't seen you here before?" Becca licked her lips and smiled so wide that she might as well have canary feathers coming out the side of her mouth.

Helena had to control herself. This woman was her employee, and they were friends to boot. Much as she wanted to, she couldn't just rip the woman off Aleksei. It was a close call though. Instead, she maneuvered her way to Aleksei's other side, grabbed him around the neck to pull his face closer and licked him nice and slow from that delicious jawline all the way up to his ear. She gave his earlobe a little nip and then took a step back.

She looked Becca straight in the eye and said, "I licked it, so it's mine."

Aleksei laughed, a good hard chuckle as Helena walked away. Becca hurried after her but didn't say anything. She knew she'd been put in her place. It happened between girls at the club all the time, but Helena had a no drama policy in place that everyone did a pretty good job of sticking too.

He was going to be one big distraction tonight. Too bad she hadn't put herself on the schedule to dance on stage. That would show him. Maybe she ought to swap with one of the other girls. But that wouldn't be fair. Center stage always raked in the cash.

She wondered if Kosta was putting Aleksei on as a regular bouncer after tonight or if this was a one-time thing. She sure would love to give him a show.

No, no. Bad girl. A strip tease for your boyfriend was not good business. She needed to get back on the floor and find her first lap dance to get her mind back on working. Not that he was her boyfriend. Fake boyfriend, nothing more.

Except for those hot as Hades kisses.

Ack. Stop thinking about that.

Helena scanned the room and found a group of guys in rumpled suits. Definitely out of town on business. Probably lonely and the perfect group to pay for lots of lap dances and drinks. She sashayed her way over to them, full well knowing all eyes in the room were watching her shake her booty.

Including Aleksei.

He'd better be drooling.

"Hey fellas. What can I get you gentlemen tonight? It's a two-fer Black Friday special on drinks and lap dances." She gave them her patented eyebrow waggle that was guaranteed to get her the sale and a good tip.

"Hell, yes. Shake that fat ass right on over here."

Sigh. It wasn't like she hadn't heard that about zillion times, yet somehow it still stung. She pretended it wasn't an insult, because she was going to take this schmoe for all his money and then demand a tip as fat as her ass. A wad of cash did a lot to soothe hurt feelings.

The bump and grind music was already going and Helena turned to give the schmoe a nice long look at the merchandise. "That's fifty dollars, honey."

"How about twenty bucks a song, sweet cheeks?"

Oh my god, was he actually negotiating with her? She put her hands on her knees and gave a couple of twerks. Some places had that as a going rate, but she was a high-end dancer and the Naughty Wolf was no two-bit joint. "Twenty bucks will get you a nice long look as I walk away. You don't want to miss out on all of this do you?"

"Maybe we should take this to the Champagne room if you want me forking over the big bucks."

Ha. With his cheap suit, with the corny owl emblazoned on the jacket, he couldn't afford her private dance rates. She was wasting her time. These guys wanted a quarter whore, not a good time worth paying for. "I don't think so, honey. How about I send over your drinks and you can catch the show on stage?"

The schmoe's friends groaned. This clearly wasn't the first time he'd nickled and dimed for entertainment. "Shut up, Earl. If you don't want to pay her, I will. Come on over to my lap, baby."

Earl socked his friend in the arm. "Fuck off. I've got the money. Here. Take it and get your ass where it belongs."

He stuffed two twenties into her g-string and slapped her

butt. Why was it the assholes were always the ones who broke the hands-off rule? One smack on the ass was nothing in the grand scheme of things. She glanced over at the bouncers who were already on their way over, but she waved them off.

They trusted that she knew what she was doing and stopped where they were. Except for Aleksei. He kept moving across the room and damn, were his eyes glowing? Must just be the lights in here.

"You got it, honey." Helena started in on her very basic lap dance routine, giving the schmoe a shimmy and a slide between his legs. She wasn't two seconds into the song when he laid both his hands on either side of her hips and yanked her down onto his lap.

"I paid good money for this."

Aleksei was right there before she could even blink. "Hands. Off. Asshole."

For a hot second all of Helena's nerves went on high alert. Half of them bristled because she could take care of herself, thank you very much. But the other half went all swoony and weak in the knees because her big, hot, sexy muscleman was here being all protective.

Dumb girly nerves.

"Watch it, tough guy. I pay your salary." Earl waved the dollar bills he'd been ready to hand over to Helena for tips during the lap dance in Aleksei's face. That was not going to go over well.

A growl was already rumbling in his chest. "You're a couple hundred short and you're going to be even shorter when I take you off at the knees for touching my...the girls. Rules say hands off."

She had to think quick if she was both going to make some money from the schmoe and his friends and get some nookie from Aleksei later. Good thing she was smarter than her hormones.

"Now boys, don't be fighting over little ole' me. As you can see, there's plenty to go around." She shook her tush in Earl's face and grabbed the tips for the lap dance right out of his fingers. Slowly, she slid the bills into her top, drawing every man's eye to her best assets.

Aleksei's eyes had that distinct blue glow around the edges that only Troikas had. Seeing it here and now in front of everyone at the club had her heart skipping a beat. Helena knew what he really was. At first she hadn't seen him as anything other than a man, but Heli's romance with Kosta had opened a whole new world of wolves and packs and claimings and matings.

She'd almost forgotten he was so much more than a mere mortal. That fact should scare her. It apparently had frightened Earl and his friends, because they all shut the hell up.

Helena found herself all hot and bothered, wanting to give this lap dance to Aleksei, even though he was butting in on her business and threatening her damn livelihood. She couldn't let that slide.

"Aleksei, love, can you ask the DJ to play some Def Leppard for me so I can show our customers the good time they just paid me for?"

"No." He crossed his arms and glared at the frightened little bunnies the group of men had become.

Sigh. She turned to Schmoe Number One and booped him on the nose. "I'll be right back, so get your lap all ready to go, honey."

Schmoe grinned all creepy like and unbuckled his pants. Whatever, after this he wasn't likely to do much with Aleksei glaring at him from across the room.

Helena grabbed Aleksei by the front of his too-tight tee and dragged him away from the table. "Look, wolf-boy. You need to calm your tits. I can deal with these assholes."

Instead of the apology or even the denial she expected from him, he said nothing. His eyes went straight to her chest when she said the word tits and that glow was back in his gaze. Was he drooling?

He was totally drooling. No way she should let him know she secretly loved that he was lusting after her. Nope. Not in a million years. She snapped her fingers to break his lust-filled stare. "Hey, eyes up here."

Aleksei's eyes snapped up and he raised one eyebrow all sexy-like. He'd known exactly what he was doing and enjoyed every second of it. He wanted her to know it too. "*Lisichka*, I know you can handle the assholes. I'm here so you don't have to. I would very much enjoy if you'd let me snap them in half so they can never look at you again."

If any other guy said anything as stupid as that, she'd be rolling her eyes and walking away. So why in the hell was it sexy as sin hearing it come out of his delicious mouth? She could damn well take care of her own independent ass. At the same time, it had her insides going all swoony that he wanted to protect her.

His protectiveness might be getting her all hot and bothered, but it didn't pay her rent. "Hey. This is a fake relationship, remember. You have no claim on me, so don't be killing my customers or scaring them off. Get a hold of youself. I gotta go. I've got a lap dance to perform. If you're so worried, watch."

Yeah, she'd just told her big fake boyfriend who was already acting ten kinds of jealous to watch her give another guy a lap dance. He was in for one hell of a show.

Helena threw one more glance over her shoulder just to make sure he was watching her saunter away from him. His gaze was firmly planted on her ass. She gave it a little extra wiggle.

The schmoes had gotten drinks in her absence. Those shots had better loosen up their wallets. "Okay, sugar. Let's get your engines revved up, shall we?"

Earl spread his legs, his belt buckle still undone and waved her over. "Get that fat ass on my dick."

It took all she had to smile. What a douchecanoe. "You mean this culo caliente, cabron?"

He probably didn't even have much of a dick for her to even sit on.

Aleksei did though. Ack. No. She should not be thinking about how big and hard and...holy crap. Now she couldn't think of anything else.

Helena spun around so the schmoe couldn't see her face, because she certainly didn't want him to think she was having carnal thoughts about his junkie-junk. She started in on her basic lap dance moves, strutting up the chair, doing a twirl and positioned herself with her ass in his face. She gave a twerk, a little shimmy and slide, but her head was not in the game.

Until she looked up and saw Aleksei staring right at her.

The guitar riffs that marked the beginning of her favorite

song to dance to filtered through the club. Oh, yes. She was ready to pour some sugar on him. In the name of love.

She locked eyes with Aleksei and all thoughts of Earl were gone from her mind. Every bump and grind she did now, was for one man alone. Aleksei Troika.

Fuck, she was in so much trouble.

YOU AIN'T NOTHING BUT A
HORNDOG

he gold short shorts Helena wore were driving him crazy, but watching her plump ass rubbing across this dickhead's crotch had him seeing red. Those damn chains dangling across the front of the barely-there leather top she had on were hypnotic and it was the only thing keeping him from going full-on wolf right here in the middle of the Naughty Wolf.

He'd like to wrap those delicate links around his hand and yank them right off. They were drawing way too much attention to her tits which were already about to fall out. Nobody but him should get to see her nipples, dammit.

Except if he did anything to interfere with her dancing, not only would she chop off his balls, she wouldn't be able to do her job. And she was damn good at her job.

He gritted his teeth and narrowed his eyes to glare at the schmoe so he knew not to even think about laying a hand on Helena again. If Aleksei had to follow her around the club all night and watch each and every one of her lap dances, well, that was a sacrifice he was willing to make. Yes. A terrible, terrible sacrifice.

He'd happily scare the patrons into tipping her well, too. His wolf growled inside, wanting to pick her up and take her away. It was not on board for watching her grind and twerk all night. The only thing the wolf wanted was to mark her, claim her, make her his mate. Right the fuck now.

The man knew he couldn't.

The man had to watch her turn another guy on, get him hard, whisper sweet nothings into his ear.

The man had to– Grr. She spun around and let the dick-head get a full view of her chest while twerking her ass right at Aleksei. His eyebrows snapped together, and he had to grind his teeth as she shoved her tits in this guy's face.

Helena danced around the chair and then put her hands on the dickhead's legs and shimmied her ass back and forth, back and forth over the guy's lap. She moaned low and her eyes fluttered shut. Was she getting turned on?

Dickhead looked up at the ceiling and groaned. "Fuck yeah, sweet cheeks. That's the way to earn your tips."

Her lids slowly re-opened and her pupils were shot with lust. But it wasn't for the asshole. Her gaze was directed straight at Aleksei. She parted her lips and licked them, so slow, until they glistened.

Dammit. She was teasing him on purpose. It wasn't like he wasn't already hard for her. It was killing him to stand here and watch her. He'd already been told off once for interfering with her job. Now she was playing with fire.

He glared at her and crossed his arms to keep from reaching for her and pulling her off the asshole's lap. His wolf pushed at her mind, even though they didn't have that connection. Yet. Aleksei mouthed the words his beast couldn't communicate. "End this. Now."

Her eyebrows shot up, but she wasn't surprised even a little because she grinned too. She kept dancing and whispered back, "Make me."

Oh, it was on. He was going to make her do a lot of things. After he spanked her ass. "Later."

His wolf wriggled in delight at these flirtations. Aleksei went from cranky to even more turned on. She was initiating a hunt, wanted him to chase her. There was very little he and his beast enjoyed more than a good chase.

He was going to chase her, and when he caught his mate they would…Aleksei's brain fritzed out at all the fantasies of having Helena on his lap, stroking her cunt, making her scream as he thrust into her.

His eyes were locked with Helena's and fuck, he was getting hard as a rock watching her. He wasn't paying attention to Earl, and that was a huge mistake.

The asshole groaned as Helena bounced on his lap and he fucking reached his god-damn hand between her legs and grabbed her crotch. "Shit, yeah—"

Earl had to die.

The wolf pushed at Aleksei and there was no stopping his beast this time. Fur sprouted from his arms and his vision went ultra-clear like 8k TV combined with night vision. He could literally see the blood pumping through the artery in Earl's throat. The one he was going to fucking rip out.

Helena's head snapped up like she could feel the anger pouring off of him. She knew Aleksei was coming for Earl. The asshole hadn't even noticed he was about to die.

No one touched his mate. No one.

Aleksei stalked toward the circle of men, his claws extended, his fangs dropped. Earl's blood would probably taste like shit. Or it would taste like victory.

Earl hooted and didn't let go of Helena. He had no idea he was about to die. Helena's eyes were wide, probably because she was smart and knew what was about to go down. Her muscles bunched up like she was preparing to join the fight.

The wolf liked that idea. Fighting side by side with his mate was a major turn on. As mates they would fight together and then fuck each other's brains out. This was going to be fun.

Helena spun and slapped Earl across the face. Then she grabbed his junk. "No. Fucking. Touching."

God that was hot. But Aleksei was going to do much worse than just grab the asshole by the balls. He'd happily rip them right off.

Earl squealed like a stuck pig and squirmed. Huh. Maybe he wouldn't get to turn Earl into a eunuch. Helena gave Earl's balls a vicious twist and the guy almost passed out. "You see that bouncer there, the one who is hulking out?"

Aleksei smash.

"He's my mother-fucking boyfriend and is going to go ballistic on your ass in about two seconds for even thinking about touching me inappropriately." She squeezed again and Earl's face went red.

The asshole jerked away from Helena's grasp and slapped her across the face. "Get off me, you fat whore."

Did Aleksei think he was angry before? No. That was kid

stuff. Now he was fucking livid. Murder. Death. Kill. The bones in his back and arms cracked as his wolf burst forth.

Aleksei Stoyanovich Troika. Stand down. The voice of the alpha of alphas, dark and rich, filtered through Aleksei's red haze of murderous intentions. Only the alpha voice of the Wolf Tzar could stop his shift and attack.

Niko stepped forward and placed an open palm on Aleksei's chest. The wolf inside receded, but growled his protest. "She is mine."

"I know, brother." Niko nodded and patted Aleksei's chest. "But you can't go around killing humans for touching her. Besides, I think your mate can take care of herself pretty damn well."

Aleksei glanced over and saw Kosta holding Helena around the waist as she was scrapping to get at Earl. She punched and kicked and scratched at his face, but Kosta dragged her away. It was like she was a wolftress and her animal was raging to get out.

"For the hundredth time, no killing the clientele, Helena." Kosta practically had to pick her up to drag her away. But being the alpha wolf he was, he encircled her with one arm and pointed at Earl. "You're lucky I was here to save you, asshole. Get the fuck out of my club. Nobody touches my girls and lives to tell the tale."

Had any other wolf, even an alpha, placed his arm around Helena and called her one of his girls, Aleksei's wolf wouldn't have been able to handle it. But this was Kosta, she was okay, his mate was unharmed. Riled up as hell, but the assholes who he'd come this close to murdering hadn't physically hurt her.

He was probably still going to kill them later.

Niko whistled, calling a few more of the extra bouncers over to make sure the trash was taken out. Aleksei wasn't the only Troika doing extra duty at the Naughty Wolf tonight and he was grateful the enforcers were here as backup. Earl should be thanking his lucky stars cooler heads were here to save his ass from getting kicked or torn apart and fed to the birds.

Good thing Kosta still had an arm holding Helena back, because she literally snarled at the group of assholes as they walked away. Fuck, that was sexy as hell.

Kosta glanced at her and grinned. "You two have had enough fun for the night. Get on out of here, Helena, and take your bodyguard home with you."

"He's not my bodyguard." The adrenaline was still pumping through her system and she was scratching for a fight.

Aleksei knew the feeling. The best way to burn off that zing of battle buzz was to get down and dirty. There was no more pretending the two of them had nothing more than this fake relationship going on. Even Kosta and Niko could see that Helena was his.

If she didn't want to take him home with her, he would throw her over his shoulder and carry her off to his cabin. Either way, he was marking and claiming her tonight.

Then he was fucking both their brains out.

Did that make him a Neanderthal Wolf? Why, yes, yes it did. If that was how he could keep his mate safe and under his protection, he was okay with that.

Helena wasn't having it. "I haven't finished my shift and I'm not letting those schmoes ruin my bottom line for the night."

Kosta did nothing more than raise an eyebrow. Not at Helena but at Aleksei. That was a 'what are you gonna do about your girl' look, if ever he'd seen one.

Fine. Over the shoulder it was. Aleksei picked Helena up caveman style with her ass right next to his face. "You let me worry about your bottom."

"Hey. You put me down. Aleksei." She squealed and kicked her feet, she even pounded on his back with her adorable fists. "You don't know squat about my bottom line."

"Oh, *lisichka*. I've had daydreams and wet dreams about this sweet ass." Just to make sure she understood exactly what kind of dreams he meant, Aleksei gave her butt a swat and let his hand linger there for a nice long time. The sooner he could get her alone, and naked, the better.

He headed straight for the door that led to the back of the house where the break room and offices were situated. He'd rather have privacy to claim his mate, but her office would have to do. This fake relationship crap was over, and he would claim her right here and right now.

When they entered the back hallway, Helena quit trying to get away. "Where do you think you're taking me?"

"Somewhere we can be alone. You and me, with nothing between us. Including your clothes." He was already having visions of pressing her up against the wall, her legs wrapping around his waist and—

"I am not getting naked with you here at work."

Well, damn. She didn't say she didn't want to get naked with him somewhere else. "Fine. I'll take you home. Then you're mine."

"Bossy much?" The tone of her voice was irritated, but the scent of her arousal was a dead giveaway.

She liked this possessive alpha side of him. It wasn't one he'd let out for a long time. But he couldn't contain it any longer. Not around her. "Yes."

"Argh. I'm not going outside in booty shorts. It's friggin' cold out there." She wriggled again trying to get down. "Let me get changed so I don't freeze to death."

Oh, yeah. He'd definitely like to watch her change. "Fine. But I make no promises about keeping my hands off you while you do."

"Horndog."

Yep. Horny wolf, anyway. Aleksei pushed into her office and slid Helena down his body, relishing every second of her lush curves pressing against his hard lines. When she was standing face to face with him, the twinkle in her eyes told him she knew exactly what he'd been doing and how much she'd enjoyed it too.

She furrowed her brows and twirled a finger at him. "Turn around. You are not watching me change."

Yes ma'am. He half turned anyway, just to appease her, but only because there was a mirror on every other wall in this room and he could see every inch of her body in the reflection no matter which way he looked. She wasn't even naked yet and his mouth was already watering.

"Hmph," Helena grumped and grabbed a sweatshirt from her locker. "I know you can see me, butthead."

Busted.

She pulled a pair of jeans on over the top of her shiny shorts. To be fair, there wasn't much more to those shorts than a pair of undies anyway. That was fine. He'd be peeling all of her clothes off in a few minutes anyway.

Helena grabbed her bag and his arm. "Come on. If I'm

being forced to take the night off, you and I are binging on Thanksgiving leftovers. And you're in charge of heating them up for me since it's your fault I didn't get pie in the first place."

"I will very happily feed you anything you want, as long as we're in bed." He was definitely thinking of all the dirtiest ways he could eat whipped cream and chocolate syrup off every inch of her body.

The refrigerator in the break room was stuffed to the brim with turkey, stuffing, pie, and the gravy Helena spilled down her front. He was going to have wet dreams about that gravy for the rest of his life. Helena rooted around on the shelves and handed him an entire feast. His arms were full in seconds. Girl after his own stomach. They could probably hole up at her place for days with this much sustenance.

Perfect.

"And bless the sweet goddess that is Heli because there is a whole pumpkin pie in here with my name on it." She stood and showed him the pie. It did actually say Helena across the top in whipped cream.

Aleksei grabbed the can of whipped cream from the door and added it to his pile. He was already imagining covering her from head to toe in it and licking every inch and curve. "This will keep us energized all night."

Helena rolled her eyes at him, but glanced from the can to his crotch and back again. Oh, ho ho. She had ideas of her own. He was totally on board for whatever she had planned and more. "Come on. I can tell you're as hungry as I am."

He waggled his eyebrows at her. "Hungry like a wolf."

They pushed out the back door of the club and Aleksei's mind was already in Helena's bedroom. If it hadn't been, he would have noticed the scent of danger wafting through the alley. This time it wasn't the mysterious lone wolf he was worried about.

"Oh, fuck me. Earl, what the hell?" Helena groaned and made a face like her pie had gone sour.

The acrid scent of revenge hung in the air around the asshole that Niko and Kosta kicked out of the club for touching Helena. Alexsei's wolf's hackles rose, and the beast pushed at his skin and psyche. No way and no how was he letting any dick, human or otherwise, near his mate.

He growled low, letting the wolf shine in his eyes. Asshole Earl didn't even seem to notice. But Helena did. She put one hand on his arm and gently squeezed.

"Aleksei, no. He's not worth it." She said a lot more with her eyes and face.

She knew who and what he was.

Aleksei had never revealed his true self to her. He didn't even know if she had seen any of his kind shift before. Wolves weren't even supposed to show themselves to humans. Well, that's the way it had been for hundreds of years. Niko and the Troikas were changing all that.

They were the reason Aleksei could even dream of being with his one true mate.

"You're worth it, *lisichka*. You're worth everything I have and more." He took her hand and kissed the back of it, because she should know she was his Queen and he would always treat her as such.

Then he turned back to Earl and let the wolf out.

He let the fur come through his skin, his bones crack and twist into a new shape, and the magic inside of him take him from man to beast in only the blink of an eye.

"Holy shit." Earl gasped.

"Holy shit is right, you schmoe. I hope he eats your face off." Helena snarled at the asshole and gave Aleksei a wink and a smile. "Howl, my wolfman, and scare this dickhead so bad he pees his pants and never wants to come back to bother us again."

Man, he loved her killer instincts. Aleksei nuzzled her hand and gave her thigh a big sloppy lick, marking his spot for later. He hadn't known for sure how she would react to seeing his true animal form. He should have known it wouldn't freak her out.

In fact, if his nose wasn't lying, she was turned on.

Fuck, yeah.

Now to take care of their unwanted visitor so he could take her home and claim his mate good and proper.

The scent of bitter fear and urine wafted over from the asshole. "Y-you, you stay the fuck away from me. I know what you are and I'm not the only one. You kill me, and my boss will come hunting your hide."

The guy was scared shitless, but he wasn't lying. He had a boss and he actually believed this person, or wolf, would avenge his death. Very interesting. It was too much of a coincidence that they were standing in the exact spot Aleksei had scented the lone wolf. Was the scent on the asshole, too?

No, his wolf would have known the second the asshole stepped into the club. But he was still connected to someone who knew about wolf-shifters, specifically the Troikas. Aleksei growled low and stalked toward Earl. He'd love to eat this guy's face off but all he really needed now was to get the scent.

Then he could pass it on to Niko, Max, and Kosta, and his duty would be done. He wasn't an enforcer. This wasn't his job anymore. His only concern now was to take care of his mate.

Which he was going to do right now. He pounced at Earl and pushed him down to the gravelly dirt. Earl tried to scramble away and whimpered a whole litany of swear words. Aleksei would laugh if he could. This dumbass deserved to know what it felt like to be the weakling.

Helena stomped over and pressed her toe of her hot AF heels into the center of his back, right over where Aleksei had ripped a gash in it. She ground her shoe into the weird tattoo of an owl between his shoulder blades. "I suggest you get the fuck out of here or my wolf is going to make you very sorry you ever even looked at me."

"You'll regret this, you whore."

Oh hell no, nobody called his woman a whore and lived to tell about it. Aleksei put his muzzle right in the guy's face and growled long and low. He allowed strings of wet wolf slobber to drip from his mouth and into the asshole's eyes.

"I'm not afraid of death, you slimy shifter. But you and your winged kin will be soon enough." Earl squirmed like worm trying to get away.

Helena made a whistling sound similar to the one a bomb made right before it crashed. Aleksei glanced up at her and she jerked her chin toward the asshole's asshole and made a biting motion with her mouth.

Ah, he liked that idea immensely. It was against a whole lot of rules for him to kill this piece of shit, but there was nothing that said he couldn't embarrass him badly enough that he'd never return.

Aleksei pounced on Earl's back, grabbed his pants with his teeth and shredded them in one giant yank. Rrriipp. Dumbass rolled, trying to get away, but all he did was expose his family jewels.

Helena pointed and broke into gales of laughter. "I thought I felt a pencil in your pocket."

Asshole scrambled away and took off running. Aleksei spit out his pants. He definitely had the guy's scent now. Blech.

He shifted back and stood completely naked in front of Helena. She glanced down and bit her lip. "Thank god. Because after that pencil dick," she held up a pinky, "I would very much like to get my hands on a..." she made a circle with her fingers spread wide, "I don't even have a good analogy for that kind of girth. Fuck me."

"Yes, ma'am."

Helena laughed and grabbed him around the neck. "I mean it. Take me home right now. That whole wolf thing is sexy as shit, and I want you so bad, I would even forgo Thanksgiving leftovers if you'll take me to bed this instant."

"No one should forgo pie. Especially when eaten directly off a body like yours."

Aleksei kissed Helena with all the lust he'd had pent up inside for days. He was taking this relationship from fake to very, very real as fast as they could.

She swatted him on the butt and broke the kiss. "I'll grab the pie, you grab your clothes. I'd much rather see them on my bedroom floor than out here in a dirty alleyway. Come on. Let's eat."

Oh, yes, he was going to eat his fill of her tonight.

EMERGENCY KITCHEN SEX

*H*elena grabbed the front of Aleksei's shirt and dragged him through the doorway of her house, slamming the big wooden door shut with her butt. She needed him like this pie needed whipped cream.

A whole hell of a lot.

She mashed their mouths together, not wanting to wait another second to feel and taste every part of him. Instead of the spicy taste of his kisses, Helena got a mouthful of turkey. "Gah. All this food is in the way and I'm about ready to dump it all on the floor just to get your tongue down my—"

Aleksei dropped the turkey and pulled her into his arms. One hand went into her hair and the other around her waist, holding her tight against his hard body. And oh, so much of it was very hard.

Pie, or Aleksei's kisses?

Why not both? She dipped her fingers into the whipped topping and smeared the sugary creaminess across his lips. He caught her fingers and drew them into his mouth, groaning so deep and low that Helena felt it all the way to her core. He sucked on her fingers hard and then flicked them with his tongue.

His eyes glowed with that supernatural blue and sparkled with so much more than desire. "Now it's my turn."

Aleksei scooped up another dollop but instead of feeding it to her, he ran his wet fingers along her throat and down the front of her cleavage as far as her sweatshirt would allow. "I'd suggest you take that off, because if you don't, in another two seconds I'm going to rip it off with my teeth."

"Honey, if there's one thing I know how to do, it's strip." She stepped away and motioned for him to follow her. "Let's put most of this food away and I'll give you a private show."

"Most?" Hunger and humor danced in his eyes.

"Oh, I'm eating this pie in the next ten minutes. Hopefully off every single naked inch of you." They weren't even down and dirty yet and she knew sex with Aleksei was going to be the best she'd had this year. Who was she kidding, it had been way longer than that since she'd gotten any action. Hell, this would make her whole decade.

He followed her into the kitchen, not giving her an inch of space. She set the leftovers on the counter and he pushed up against her from behind. "Only if I get to eat you for dessert."

God, this was going to be so hot. But somehow it was also fun to get each other all wound up. Sex for Helena wasn't usually...fun. Flirty and dirty, sure. Hot and heavy, yep. But fun? Not in as long as she could remember. "I'm counting on it."

She spun in his arms, intending to kiss and tease and grind up against him, but Aleksei had other plans. He grabbed her around the waist and lifted her so she was sitting on the counter. Then he pushed himself between her legs, forcing her to spread them wide to accommodate his huge body.

She hoped he was huge everywhere. If the bulge in his jeans was any indication, she was going to be one happy and satisfied lady.

"Helena, I want this to be good for you." He was exactly the right height that his cock was already aligned with her pussy. He ground against her and she damned herself for putting these jeans on. "But my wolf is howling for me to take you right here, right now."

"Then take me, because while I don't have a wolf to push me, my girly bits are screaming for your attention."

With one hand he grabbed for the fastening of his jeans and with the other he palmed her head, gripped her hair, and tugged, sending shockwaves of sensations through her scalp down her spine. He scraped his teeth across her throat and she arched her back, gasping at the feel of his teeth on her skin.

God, they didn't even have their clothes off yet and she was this close to coming. There was something about the idea of him biting her that had her system ready to overload, so much so that she shoved her fingers into his hair and held his head so his mouth was against her pulse point. It beat, beat, beat beneath his lips and she could feel the same pounding between her legs.

"I need you Aleksei, need this."

The rumble of his growl sent her pulse into overdrive. Why was that such a damn turn on?

"*Zhin moya*, do you know what it means to be mated to one of my kind, to a wolf shifter?"

According to Heli, it meant incredible sex at all hours of the day or night. It also meant a commitment for life. Did she want that? She'd never relied on anyone else, never counted on someone to be around for more than however long it took to get what they needed from her. That scared place in her mind that had been hurt so many times before cowered away from the idea.

A newer, stronger part of her bloomed where the scared bit had been. This was a happy Helena, with all the excitement of newfound love sending the shadows of fear away with its light of hope. All the same, she couldn't totally trust this hopeful hunger inside of her. It had been known to lead her astray before.

"Just because we have mind-blowing sex and eat pie off each other doesn't mean we have to mate for life right this second, does it? Can we fuck each other senseless now and figure out the rest later?" To entice him to say yes, she reached between them and shoved the waistband of his jeans down his hips.

Ooh, going commando. Delicious and something she'd remember. She already had visions of dragging him into the backroom at work and shoving her hands down his pants. Why imagine it, when she could do whatever she wanted right now? Helena wrapped her fingers around his cock and stroked her nails up his shaft and back down.

He groaned and buried his face in the crook of her neck. "You are going to kill me."

"In all the best ways." If there was one thing she knew how to do well, it was how to distract a horny guy from whatever else was on his mind.

"But two can play at your game, *lisichka*." Aleksei held up one hand and his fingernail lengthened into a sharp talon. With a couple flicks of his wrist he sliced every seam of her jeans open and the material fell right off her body.

"Ha. Bet you forgot I was wearing these shiny gold booty sho—" Before she could even finish her sentence her shorts fell off into shreds and she was bare to the world. "Hey, those were my work clothes."

Aleksei grinned and licked his lips. "You probably should learn not to wear any panties around me. Because they won't last long."

Oh, he wanted to get all dominant and bossy? That was hot as hell, but he wasn't allowed to make demands of her without letting her have rules of her own. "Fine, then you can't wear shirts around me so that I can ogle your chest and shoulders to my heart's content. Time to strip, sex-ay Aleksei."

The blue fire of the wolf glowed in his eyes but there was also humor there. He was enjoying this battle to be on top as much as she was. Aleksei whipped his shirt over his head, but he wasn't prepared for her next move.

Helena grabbed a handful of the pumpkin pie and smacked him square in the chest with it. His eyes went wide with surprise and he froze. Helena had to work hard to hold in her guffaw at his expression. She knew how to fix that face. With one finger she swiped a line through the pump-kiny goo and brought the treat to her mouth. Her tongue darted out to swirl and taste the pie, then she sucked the end of her finger and made all the appropriate porn noises to accompany her little show.

Aleksei's mouth dropped, his eyes trained on her finger. A quick glance down showed he and his cock were imagining everything she could do with her mouth. She was just getting started.

"What? I wanted a taste. You know I've been fantasizing about pie. And you. So why not combine them and get everything my—" She'd almost said heart desired. They weren't ready to admit love. Right now, she would keep it light and sexy. Even if she was falling for him. Hard.

"—everything I want, all in one delicious, sexy package." This time instead of using her finger, Helena went straight to the source and licked from his sternum up right to that soft spot in his throat.

She wasn't prepared for what Aleksei did next. He growled and groaned at the same time, then picked her up at the waist, spun and laid her out across her kitchen table. He crawled up over her and spread her thighs with his knees. "You're the delicious one, and you make me so hungry for you I'm losing my damn mind."

Thank God she had a freaking sturdy wooden table.

She wrapped her legs around the back of Aleksei's thighs and ground against him making both hers and his eyes roll back in their heads. "We can go back to foreplay and pieplay later, I want you now. Grab a condom, they're in the silver-ware drawer."

"I will if you really want me to, but we don't need it."

Sigh. All guys thought that. Then they put one on if they wanted to be with her. "We do. I'm keeping us both safe."

She expected more of a fight with him about it, but he slid off the table, taking her with him. She loved that he couldn't bear to let her go, and she wrapped her legs tighter around his hips. He pressed her against the counter and yanked every drawer within reach open. "Why in the world do you have condoms in your kitchen?"

"For emergency kitchen sex." Sort of. In the last few years, those condoms had been wishful thinking. They'd ended up in the drawer during a tidying binge she'd gone on after one too many episodes of Marie Kondo's show on Netflix.

"Got 'em." He dumped the entire contents on the counter and plucked one from the pile. She watched him go for his mouth like he was going to rip it open with his teeth and snatched it from him. Wouldn't do to have the thing rip before he even got it on.

She carefully opened the wrapper and handed him the condom. Nothing hotter than watching a guy roll on protection. Sounded funny, but because it was important to her, she was turned on when a guy did it, especially without question. Plus, the anticipation of being with him was that much closer.

He looked at the condom, looked down at his erection and his eyebrows went up. Helena almost giggled, but thought better of it. No man wanted his cock laughed at. "Sorry, didn't know I'd need the XXL size."

Aleksei let out a quick chuckle and then began to roll the teeny tiny bit of latex. He got it maybe a fourth of the way on and it split right down the middle. "Shit. Gimme another one."

Helena grabbed another, but this one didn't fare much better. It went flying over her shoulder and splatted against the backsplash. "Fuck. Let me try again."

Uh. Why did she have the distinct feeling he'd never done this before? "Allow me, sugar."

No way she believed he was a virgin. Nope, not a chance. There were men out there who'd never worn a condom before, but would he so readily agree if he had that big of a problem wearing them? No. It simply had to be because these ones were smaller than what he'd usually buy for himself. She didn't want him feeling self-conscious about any of this, so she'd make this act a bit of foreplay.

She gently dragged her nails from the base of his cock to the tip, teasing him with her touch, giving a hint of what could be pain if she pressed a smidgen more. His dick grew incredibly harder and larger under her touch and she licked her lips. Oh, how she wanted to taste him.

Which gave her a great idea. Helena gave him a shove back and dropped off the counter and onto her knees.

"Helena, baby, our fun and games are going to be over if your mouth comes anywhere near my cock."

She'd love to really see him lose control like that. But she'd save that bit of fun for later. She looked up at him and winked. "Then we'll just cover each other in pie and spend the rest of the night eating."

Just one taste of him, then she'd roll the condom on, with her mouth. A party trick she'd learned in college. She licked the drop of pre-cum forming on the tip of his cock and swirled her tongue around the head. Aleksei groaned and grabbed the edge of the counter.

"Fuck. You're going to kill me."

In all the best ways.

She really wanted to take all of him in her mouth, hear him groan and growl some more and make him come for her. But she also wanted him deep inside of her making her growl and groan. She popped the condom between her lips and rolled the first inch on.

The countertop behind her head creaked and cracked under Aleksei's hands. "Goddess above, your mouth is so good. Give me more, *lisichka*."

If she wasn't so anxious to ride him like a stripper on a pole, she's pull this condom off, cover him in whipped cream and suck him until he howled at the moon. Next time. They had plenty of leftover pie to spread all over each other. But since her pussy was practically quivering in anticipation, she used her lips and her fingers to roll the protection on, giving him only the tiniest taste of what she could do with her mouth.

The moment she popped him out from between her lips, he yanked her up and laid her back out on the table. "I hope you like it rough, baby, because I'm going to fuck you till you see stars."

He threw her ankles up onto his shoulders and pushed into her with one long, hard thrust.

Helena threw her head back and closed her eyes, loving the feeling of being so filled by him. "Yes, Aleksei, fuck me hard. I need you to make me come."

She needed more from him than that, but didn't know how to express the tingling of feelings creeping up from her core to her heart.

Aleksei thrust with fast, hard strokes, hitting her in just the right places. Their frenzied fucking was surprisingly perfect. For once she didn't need all the foreplay, the antici-pation, the long drive to orgasm. She couldn't normally come without a lot of dirty talk and hands or a tongue on her clit.

Sex with her hungry wolf was so much more than anything she'd ever done before. This was more sensual, more erotic, and exactly what would push her over the edge in mere minutes. Her body was already flying, but she needed something more.

She pried her eyes open, wanting to see his face, connect with him, watch him lose control. When she looked up at Aleksei, his eyes glowed a deep blue and his fangs dropped, pressing at the edges of his mouth. The sight of his teeth sent a thrill from the top of her spine all the way down to the base. Her mouth watered and she licked her lips.

She wanted those teeth on her more than she wanted her next breath, more than she needed the oncoming orgasm. "Bite me, Aleksei, bite me now."

BETTER THAN PIE

*H*elena was killing him. Her hot, greedy cunt clenched around his cock, not wanting to let him go. With each thrust, her breasts bounced and pert nipples teased him, begging to be sucked. He didn't dare or he wouldn't be able to resist nibbling his way up her chest to her soft, exposed throat.

He'd never felt or seen anything as fantastic as her body begging him to take her in all the ways he could imagine.

His wolf howled inside, pushing at him to mark her, claim her, make her his forever. This electricity between them was more intense than any other connection he'd ever known. It was more than chemistry. It was pure magic.

He'd known already that she was his true mate, but being with her like this sent his soul into a frenzy, needing to complete their bond. His teeth ached to scrape across her skin, sink into her flesh, and bite her. His heart hurt with the wanting, the waiting.

No way she actually wanted him to bite her. She didn't

know what she was asking, what it truly meant. But Goddess, how could he not?

"Not yet, love. First you have to come for me." That was a lie straight from the pits of hell. If the Troika boys were to be believed, biting his mate to mark her would give them both the best pleasure of both of their lives. He couldn't risk it.

Aleksei would simply have to make her come over and over without marking her, so that she was well satisfied and forgot all about her request. A growl escaped from the depths of his chest. His wolf didn't like that idea at all. His fangs had already dropped, and he could practically taste her erotic flavor, feel her orgasm getting closer, know that their souls were becoming one.

How could he ever deny that?

The sooner he made Helena come, the better. Being inside of her like this and having her begging him to make her his in every way, had his tight rein on his control slipping away fast and hard.

Dear God, he was going to give in. He was going to give her everything she wanted, He was going to destroy them both.

Fuck, fuck, fuck. He couldn't do this, not to his perfect, beautiful, smart, strong mate. He couldn't saddle her with the mountains of trash he'd piled on his own soul.

He had to protect her, if only from himself.

"Aleksei, please, I'm so close. I need you. All of you."

He would give her only the best of him, the part that knew how to please his woman. Her ankles were still on his shoulders, which gave his cock all the access to her plump pussy, but her thighs hid her clit from him. Aleksei grabbed her calves and dropped her feet to his waist, spreading her thighs and exposing the heaven awaiting him.

"I'm going to make you come so hard you won't even remember your own name," He pulled his dripping cock from her wet cunt, noticed that the stupid condom was in shreds, ignored that fact, and dropped his face to her sweet core.

He'd scented her arousal the whole night, but now she filled his senses with the ripe fruity aroma of her need. There was no mustiness of reticence, no bitter almond essence of a hidden agenda. She was pure golden raspberries, open in both body and mind to him.

Aleksei's heart stopped beating, overwhelmed with awe at her open vulnerability. She was so purely herself with him and she deserved the same of him. His chest pounded from the inside out as his heart came back from its frozen death, as if it approved of his resolve to find a way through his own darkness and be worthy of such an amazing woman as a mate.

He scraped his teeth across the sensitive skin of her pussy lips and then licked them to soothe the sting. Helena bucked beneath him until he held her still with one hand and slipped two fingers inside her wet heat. A moment later he licked up her slit and swirled his tongue around her clit. The taste of her exploded into his mouth sending his wolf so close to the surface he almost bit her cunt and put his mark on her in the most intimate of places.

He would mark her. He would find a way to get his head out of his ass and be worthy of her. But not tonight. He wouldn't mark her simply because he lost control. He would claim her under the full moon in the sacred circle, as was the way of every generation of wolves before him. Tonight was about pleasing his woman.

Helena pushed her hands into his hair and held him tight. Her lust swirled around them both, the most potent aphrodisiac. Aleksei curled his fingers and found just the right spot to drive her over the edge. He tickled her g-spot and sucked her clit between his teeth teasing the sensitive bud with flicks of his tongue.

Her moans went from languorous to impatient and needy. "Yes, Aleksei, right there. Oh my god, I'm going to come so hard. Oh god. Yes."

He had a dark desire to tell her she couldn't come until he told her to, but loved even more the knowledge that she'd tell him to go fuck himself if he did. Goddess, he loved her smart mouth. He loved her.

Shit. He. Loved. Her.

This was more than just her being his fated mate, his frayed and tattered heart was being stitched back together because of Helena. His Helena.

Aleksei redoubled his efforts, wanting so badly to see her come for him, only for him. His wolf still wasn't happy that he wasn't marking and claiming her, but it too wanted to please Helena above all else. He found himself nipping at her sweet flesh more than simply teasing her and man, oh man, did she love that.

Her fingers gripped his hair, pulling at his scalp, sending tingles across his skin. Helena cried out, screaming his name and pushing her hips forward. "Aleksei, yes, yes, Aleksei."

Her body convulsed, her clit pulsated against his teeth and tongue, and her pussy clenched around his fingers as she came. Her orgasm was magic to his soul. His wolf howled in his head declaring his dominance over her body.

One word repeated through his mind over and over with each breath. Mine.

Helena was his, and soon he would explain to her everything it meant to be the true mate of a wolf, how it would change both their worlds. He would let her choose for herself. Regardless of what she decided, she was his and would be for evermore.

With one more lap of his tongue, he withdrew his fingers and stood. Helena's body glistened and she breathed hard, her eyes bright with a new glow sparkling just for him. She was the most beautiful thing he'd ever known in his life. He swooped her up into his arms and turned toward the entry to the kitchen intent on taking her to bed.

"Wait. grab the pie. If we're doing more of that, we're going to get hungry."

He swung around so Helena could snag the pie. "Get the whipped cream too."

"Oh, I'm going to cover you from head to toe, and lick every inch." She gave the nozzle a little squirt and licked the cream right off the tip.

"That sounds like an excellent plan. But I get to go first." He gave the top of the can of whipped cream a flick of his own tongue.

Helena snatched it away. "No way, it's not your turn and I'm in recovery after that orgasmpalooza you just laid on me."

"Palooza? Yes. I like that. We'll have all the orgasm-paloozas tonight, again tomorrow, and at least for three more days after that. Then I'll need to go back to guarding you."

"You're hilarious." She said that deadpan and with so much sarcasm he could taste it in the air.

Later he would explain the danger from the lone wolf, and how it was his duty to protect her from now on. He stepped through the doorway of Helena's bedroom and laid her out on the plush bed covered in a thick faux fur blanket with extra furry pillows. She set the pie on the nightstand but kept the squirty whipped cream close at hand.

Aleksei's list of discussion topics was growing and not having her know the important information about his world as it pertained to her role in his life and her safety made his skin itch. Particularly in the groin area.

Or maybe that was the remains of the condom still dangling from his cock.

"I am? I thought I was rather sexy." He waggled his eyebrows at her.

Helena giggled, which was adorable. He'd never seen her do that before. She was sensual and serious, but she hadn't laughed like this, so free and herself.

"You are definitely sexy. But I've never had so much fun with anyone like I am with you." She reached up and ran her thumb across his bottom lip. Aleksei sucked it into his mouth and swirled his tongue around and around the same as he'd done to her clit. Her eyes sparkled and grew darker with each pass.

"There's more condoms in the nightstand, and some toys, if you're up for it." She pointed to the drawer with her can.

Toys. Was he up for it? Was. He. Up. For. It? His cock definitely was. He was already feverishly imagining what she did here in her fur-covered bed with those toys. "Lemme just get rid of the remnants of this piece of shit broken condom."

Helena's eyes dropped to where his hand was ripping the stupid little bits of latex crap off his dick. "It broke? Is that why you went down on me?"

He tossed the remains into the tiny trash can next to the nightstand. "No. I've wanted to do that since the day we first met, and I want to do it again right now. You're fucking delicious."

She rolled her eyes like she didn't believe him. He'd show her exactly how much he meant that. "Just tell me you're clean."

If she wanted him to wear a condom, he would. If she wanted him to wear a one-eyed one-horned flying purple people eater while he fucked her, he would. But she didn't need to worry about diseases. "If that's what you're worried about, then let me reassure you. Wolf shifters don't get human diseases. We don't get sick, not the in the ways you do. I swear you're safe with me."

"Wait, what? For real? Not sick in anyway? Like you haven't ever had the flu or the chicken pox or anything?"

"I swear it. Although I have no idea why a chicken would put a pox on you. What did you ever do to the chicken?" Humans were weird. He'd grown up on the fringes of their world, and until Niko and Selena had started their revolution to allow wolves to choose their own mates, their fated mates, he'd stuck to socializing mostly with his own kind.

He'd had one human girlfriend before, but she was nothing like his Helena.

His.

She was his through and through and he would never let her go.

She laughed again and threw her hands up in the air. "Why did no one tell me this?"

Aleksei crawled across the bed, taking his time, kissing her ankle, then the side of her knee, then her inner thigh. "I tried."

Or at least he'd meant to.

"Next you'll tell me I don't have to worry about getting pregnant either."

He chuckled and kissed her mound, teasing her by not going where he knew she wanted him. "You don't. Not unless it's a full moon and you bear my mark."

Helena sat bolt upright. "You're making that up."

"Someday, I'll take you to the sacred circle under the full moon and you can witness for yourself that magic the Goddess bestows upon us." But not yet, not tonight, and not until they were both ready. "I assure you, while I'd love to see your belly ripe with my child, tonight is only about you and me having a lot of sex...and pie. Lots of pie."

Aleksei snagged the can of whipped cream from her and circled each of her lush tits with the sweet goop, then dotted her nipples. They looked like eyes staring up at him, begging to be kissed. Just because he felt like it, he drew a crescent moon across her lower belly. Not until he was finished did he realize he'd drawn a giant smiley face in whipped cream on her tawny skin.

Maybe because he actually felt happy for the first time since the death of his alpha. He was whole again, being here with his one true mate. She made his dark places not feel quite so bleak with the light of her love, her smile, her strength, and her luscious body that was all his. His.

It would still be hard for him not to mark and claim her, but he was done holding himself back. When they'd crashed together in the hallway and the kitchen, it had been the pure adrenaline of needing to fuck each other's brains out. This time, he'd be making love to her. Giving his body to her as she gave hers to him.

Helena sensed his change in mood, grabbed his face and pulled him in for a long, soul-deep kiss. This one was slow, and sensual. Their mouths met, their tongues teased with light caresses that became hotter and more fervent with each second they were fused together.

She broke the kiss well before he was ready and moved to her knees so they were chest to chest. Aleksei swiped the cream from her breasts and fed it to her, then pinched her nipples to get the last bits and sucked them into his mouth. They came together again for more kisses, Helena wrapping her arms around his neck, and he didn't care that their abdomens would be sticky.

"I want to make love to you, Aleksei. Nothing between us, no more games. Just you inside me, making each other feel good. I want to look deep into your eyes when you come in me, and I want you to hold me tight against you as I come on your cock. Can we do that?"

She asked so sweetly, but this was no request. This was a demand that he give himself to her fully this time. "We can do that for—"

He almost said forever. He wanted to. He would someday soon. "—as long as you want and need me, *zhin moya.*"

Helena's smile came all the way from her heart, maybe

even her soul. She pushed Aleksei back so he was seated, and then straddled his lap. "It's my turn to make you feel good first."

She sank down onto his erection and it took all he had not to throw his head back and bark to the moon that he had found his own personal goddess. He did let out a low approving growl.

"I love it when you go all wolfy on me. Growl for me again, and let me see those sexy-ass fangs." Fully seated on him, she squeezed her inner muscles and threw her own head back, enjoying this as much as he was.

Aleksei's fangs were already out and he licked his tongue across them, staring at her bared throat. He grabbed her hips and moved her up and down on his cock, thrusting into her.

The muscles in her legs tensed. "I'm not too heavy for you, am I? I figured you were big enough that I wouldn't squish you. I wouldn't normally try this, but..."

"Look at me and listen, because I want you to understand. You're perfect. Making love to you like this is the best fucking thing ever. I love that you're tough and strong and I don't feel like I'm going to break you. You are my every wet dream and fantasy come to life. I'm the one who needs to worry that I won't be man enough for you. Don't ever think you're too much woman for anyone."

Helena closed her eyes as if his words gave her as much pleasure as his body. He hoped that they did. When she opened them again, she moved her hips faster, sliding up and down on his cock. Every move she made had him so close to coming that he had to grit his teeth to keep from coming.

She would always come first. Always.

In a few more thrusts her breathing spiked and her nipples pebbled. Her legs were trembling and Aleksei took over, lifting her and dropping her back down, jerking his hips so she would feel him deeper inside her than any other man in her life before. Her eyes fluttered shut and she bit her bottom lip.

"Look at me, Helena. I want to see your eyes when you come."

When she stared down at him, the blue glow from his wolf reflected back in her own eyes. It took his breath away to see a glimpse of what she would look like as a wolf and it was more than he could handle.

"*Ya lyublyu tebya, zhin moya, Ya lyublyu tebya.*" He slipped into Russian to tell her he loved her, and together they both came, staring into each other's eyes.

Helena didn't say she loved him back. She likely had no idea he'd just splayed his heart out for her anyway. She bit her lips and groaned low until her body locked and it took her breath away. Then she collapsed forward onto him and buried her head in his shoulder.

He'd never felt so incredibly connected to anyone in his life.

Together they breathed hard, the beat of their hearts and lungs matching each other's rhythms. When Helena wriggled on his lap, he realized she wasn't going anywhere. Not only were their souls locked together, their bodies were, too.

His wolf had made its own claim on her body with the bulge of his knot at the base of his cock. He wouldn't be able to pull out until the wolf was satisfied she was thoroughly his. Not that he minded this instinctive ritual from his beast within. It gave him more time to be close to her, one with her.

Aleksei gently laid back so Helena was spread out on top of him and rolled them to their sides with her leg thrown over his hip. "I want to hold you like this all night, love."

She snuggled tight and her reply came out drowsy and contented. "I'm glad you didn't just pull out. I like the feeling of still being connected with you."

Ah, so his wolf knew what it was doing after all.

He held her tight until she quietly fell asleep. Only when she was peaceful and resting in his arms did the knot subside. He hated to break their connection, but he did, knowing they would be one again soon.

Aleksei drifted off to sleep with her scent wrapping him in a welcoming warmth he'd never known. He awoke again a few moments later, the bitter scent of betrayal. loss and fear tainting the air.

The lone wolf howled from right outside Helena's house.

THE NOTHING

*W*hat the fuck was that?

Aleksei was an animal in bed. Not literally. Although Helena's heart rate and lust skyrocketed the second he brought out those wolf fangs. Holy saints above, the way he scraped his teeth across her skin was so fricking sexy, she thought she'd orgasm from that one touch alone.

Now they were snuggled up in her bed and he'd done the one thing she craved after sex but never got. He'd stayed buried deep inside of her. Dudes were always pulling out and waving their dicks around before she was even done coming, if she got to come at all. She wanted to snuggle, to continue to feel close to him, be connected both spiritually and physically for a little while longer.

God, this was heaven. Plus there was still that pie to be smeared all over him and eaten back up.

She loved pie.

She also loved Aleksei.

Yep. Loved. She was head over heels for this grumpy guy who she was just supposed to be having a fake relationship with to get through the holidays without being harassed. Something had changed between them tonight. They'd gone from something superficial and convenient, to sexy as fuck, to an open and deep link that felt as if it went all the way down to her soul.

This must be what Heli was talking about when she got all mushy and gooey about Kosta. Did it have something to do with his wolf nature? Were there supernatural forces at work to make her feel this way? Naw. That was ridiculous. Her feelings were her own. Nothing could take away the happiness and joy fluttering around her chest like a flipping butterfly on rainbow steroids.

She snuggled deeper into his arms, loving the warmth of his chest against her cheek and his cock nestled in her pussy. She felt so full, in her heart and in places down below. She sighed and let herself fall into the most comfortable sleep of her life.

Helena dreamed of running through a forest, the Reserve at the edge of town. The dirt was cool beneath her feet, but she wasn't cold even with the wind whipping across her face. Something warm and furry wrapped around her keeping her safe. She was free and alive like never before.

But there was something evil in the woods. She could smell it. The scent was like pure vodka burning her nose. Eyes peered at her from the shadows. These weren't filled with the strong blue glow like Aleksei's wolf, they were an abyss, darkness, the absence of light.

A wolf the color of darkest storm clouds emerged from the underbrush and stalked toward her. His growl hit her full in the chest like the rumble of thunder. His teeth gnashed like lighting. But his dark gaze wasn't directed at her.

Oh no. He was after Aleksei.

"*Lisichka*, wake up and don't make a sound. Shhh." Aleksei's deep voice pulled Helena from sleep. Pulling her from a dream that had suddenly turned into a nightmare.

His tone wasn't soft and soothing, but filled with foreboding, and he held her tight to his chest to keep her silent, not to hush her scared cries leftover from the dreamworld. Every muscle in his body was tense, spring loaded, ready to pounce. What in the hell was going on?

She looked up, trying to ask him with her eyes to tell her what was wrong. His had that beautiful blue glow of his wolf. But his gaze was not on her. Instead he peered through her window into the gloomy, almost-winter night.

"Do you have a security system?"

She shook her head. Rogue wasn't the kind of place where anyone had fancy security and cameras at their house. Heck, sometimes she didn't even remember to lock her door. Was someone trying to break in? Aleksei could just shift and take them out. Okay, then, worse than a burglar.

A scrape of nails across the side of her house followed by a haunting growl told her everything she needed to know in an instant. Aleksei wasn't the only wolf at her house. Whoever or whatever was outside was dangerous.

"Where's your phone?"

Damn, it was probably in the hall where they'd dropped most of their stuff in their hurry to get each other's clothes off. Helena pointed out the bedroom door and hooked her wrist to indicate the front of the house.

"Okay. I'm going to shift, and you're going to run and find your phone. Call Niko or Max and tell them to get to your house right away, that the lone wolf is here and I need backup. Got it?"

She nodded, ready to rock and roll or get the hell out of dodge or whatever just do it phrase would get her through this.

Aleksei slipped the covers to the side and tugged her to a crouching position on the floor. "Everything is going to be okay, love. I will protect you with my life."

"Be careful of the wolf with the Nothing eyes." She was supposed to be keeping silent, but that warning had popped out as if she wasn't in control of her own mouth. Whoa.

The wolf's eyes called up exactly the image, and churning of fear, of the foreboding cloud of destruction from classic *The NeverEnding Story* kids' movie. Darkness, despair, and death, bearing down on them. Or rather it had already come for him.

"You saw him?"

Uh, only in a dream. "Not exactly."

She blinked, seeing the vision of the monster and his tormented eyes in her mind again. That's when the shaking started. She wasn't cold, but her teeth chattered and a shiver ran through her body as if she was on the verge of hypothermia. She closed her eyes for just a second to get her bearings and the dream popped back into her mind as if she'd fallen back asleep.

The grey wolf crouched and pounced straight toward her, leaping straight over her head and toward Aleksei behind her.

"Nooo..." The cry resonated only in her mind. She

101

couldn't get the words to come out of her mouth. Her jaw felt strange, as if it had been elongated, and her teeth poked down like long canines, or even fangs. She tried again and this time her lungs and vocal cords were on board but what came out of her mouth was a howl, not words.

She choked back the sound and whipped around to follow the arc of the wolf's jump. She tensed her muscles to run and block him if she could, but she wasn't fast enough. He touched down like a fricking ballerina, right next to Aleksei, and bounded ahead. Red eyes appeared, staring back at the trio, and a pack of mangy brown wolves stepped out of the darkness.

With all of her heart, Helena knew these wolves were there to kill them all.

The grey wolf attacked them with such ferocity she cowered for a moment. This beast was a killing machine, but not a monster. He slaughtered the other wolves with the grace of a God-damned furry ninja.

Aleksei joined in the fray but was thrown to the ground by the biggest of the enemy wolves. Blood soaked the ground beneath him and he lay so still that Helena couldn't move either. Huge gashes were torn in the fur at his throat.

Aleksei, don't you dare fucking die on me. She ran to his side but was stopped halfway there by another of the mangy mutts. It snapped its jaws at her and if she didn't know better, she thought it smiled in that creepy serial killer who wants to have your liver with some fava beans way.

In a flash, Aleksei was on the creepy wolf's back, tearing at his opponent's fur, raking his claws across the throat. He glanced at Helena for only a second and his voice burst into her mind.

Run.

"Helena, Helena. Can you hear me?" Someone shook her arms frantically. "Fuck, Helena come back to me."

"I'm here." She forced her eyes open and stared at Aleksei's throat for a full count of three to be sure it was intact before she looked up at him. She swallowed, trying to get her dry mouth to open and say something about what she'd seen. "If you go and die on me, I'm going to kill you."

Yeah, yeah. That didn't make sense. She couldn't shake the feeling that this dream was not simply her imagination. "Or I'll become a ghostbuster and trap you in a metal box and keep you at the fire station."

"Shh, shh. I'm not going to die. But I love that you'd reverse haunt me if I did. Same, babe, same." He whispered and kissed each of her eyelids. "Now we have to go, if you're up for it. Actually, we need to get out of here even if you're not okay. There's something very dangerous outside and I need to make sure you're safe."

The grey wolf. "Oh. He's on our side. I think. I'm pretty sure. I don't know. The vision made it seem that way. It's a little confusing."

"You had a vision? Shit. Damn. Fuck. I gotta get you to Zara and Heli, they'll know what to do. You're friends with Heli, aren't you? Got her number?"

She did. How would sweet Heli be able to help? Chocolate chip cookie them to death? Probably he meant Zara and Heli would hang with her while the boys went out to fight off the big bad wolf, who was big, but not bad. Eyeroll.

Helena had spent her whole life taking care of herself. She wasn't going to stop now just because she had a werewolf for a boyfriend. "I've got a baseball bat in the front hall closet. Let's just go out there and kick these guys' butts, like we did that schmoe."

"This isn't the same thing at all, my badass mate. If these wolves are one-bloods, they're extremely dangerous." He glanced out the window and ushered her closer to the doorway and the hall. "They'll eat your baseball bat for a snack. I don't even want to think about what they'll do to you. I hate that I've dragged you into pack problems, but I won't let anything happen to you."

A. She didn't know what a one-blood was, but it sounded disgusting, and B. This conversation was not going the way she wanted it to. As of tonight, they were a team. At least she'd thought they were. She'd given her heart and soul to him. She hadn't meant to, hadn't planned to, in fact, she'd told both him and herself that this didn't have to be serious.

It wasn't a lie at the time, but she'd been so very wrong.

But maybe he didn't feel that way. Or maybe she'd made him think she wasn't ready for him to feel that way. Yeah, probably that one. She was great at that particular skill. She'd been pushing people she loved away her whole life. She didn't want to push him away. Out of anyone in the whole wide world, she wanted to pull Aleksei to her and keep him there.

Forever.

"Aleksei, you need to tell me right now if everything that happened between the two of us tonight meant something to you or not." Yes or no. Don't say no.

The scratching at the window sounded again and Aleksei inserted himself between her and the intruders. "Now is not the time to talk about our relationship."

"Our fake relationship?" She did her best not to sound

like a clingy, needy woman asking these questions. She'd never been either in her entire life. She wasn't starting now. Because she wouldn't believe for a second that what they'd become was fake. It never was for her, even if she'd lied to herself and said it was.

If he said no now, she was going to fight for him. She'd rather fight alongside him against the monsters outside.

His head snapped back from his view of the window and he grabbed her face between his hands. "Fuck. No. Dammit. It's been all I could do all night long not to mark you and claim you as my mate. You're mine, Helena, and I'm yours."

Thank God. She clasped her hands over his and gave them a squeeze. "Good. That's what I thought. We're in this together and you're not shipping me off to the convent now."

Even in this moment where something unknown was knocking at their door and she knew he was worried about protecting her, he smiled in a way that went all the way to his eyes and took her breath away. "Never the convent. I think it might erupt into flames with the heat of our lust for each other if we even got close."

Aww.

Now they could kick some ass and take some names. Together.

Something slammed against the side of the house so hard the lamp on her bedside table fell over and toppled to the floor. A ruckus that sure as hell sounded like the worst kind of dogfight erupted right outside. Time to get that baseball bat. And maybe call animal control. Or the Troikas. Or both.

"Love, call Heli, quickly. Tell her to send Kosta and any

other Troika, Grimm, Bay, or Serenity Enforcers here to your house."

"What are you going to do while I call for backup?"

"I'm going to hold them off."

"What can I do to help?"

The twitch in his eye told her he didn't want her anywhere near the danger, but that he was trying his best to honor that she wasn't going to back down. "After you've made that phone call, get the bat and keep it at the ready. If I need to, I'll retreat back into the house. You can clobber anyone who tries to follow me in."

It wasn't exactly taking action, but she knew he was trying. Plus, they really did need some backup. That fight was getting worse, and soon the Troikas and their friends weren't the only ones who would be showing up. The police were probably already on their way.

Hadn't Heli mentioned that the Sheriff's department was staffed with shifters, though? If she couldn't get hold of Heli and Kosta, she'd call the Sheriff himself. There ought to be a 9-1-1 for shifter emergencies too. She'd suggest that tomorrow.

What she could only guess was the body of a wolf slammed against her house again. That was her signal. Helena took off running down the hall, naked as the day she was born. The glass in her bedroom window shattered, scaring the bejeesus out of her and spiking her adrenaline. She made it to the front hallway in about two seconds flat.

Helena grabbed her bag from the floor where she'd dropped it and dumped out the contents. A bag of make-up, her wallet, sunglasses, breath mints, her Kindle, a handful of receipts, an emergency pair of undies, eyedrops, and a nail file all fell out, but no cell phone. After a full minute of shoving the detritus around, her phone was still nowhere to be found. Dammit. She must have left it at the club.

Why, oh why, did she get rid of her landline? Who cared if she hadn't called anyone on it in years, she was getting that reinstalled tomorrow. Aleksei was going to freak out when she told him they couldn't call for backup.

She grabbed his shirt from the pile of clothes on the floor and pulled it on over her head. It was long enough that it went to the tops of her thighs. Not the best idea to go swinging a baseball bat at attacking wolves naked. Hmm...unless that would distract them.

She did have great tits.

Along with the bat from the closet, she also picked up the little metal nail file. If the TSA didn't want something like this on a flight, then it was a good enough weapon for her. She could probably poke someone's eye out with it. Or shove it up their nose and scramble their brains.

As quietly as possible, she crept back down the hall to the bedroom. But when she got there, the bedroom wasn't a bedroom.

It was a war zone.

SAVE THE STRIPPER, SAVE THE WORLD

*F*ucking one-bloods.

Aleksei thought they were finally rid of these scum of the earth when Niko had become the Wolf Tzar.

Wrong.

He guessed they hadn't all changed their ways and seen the light. Nope. They must have gone into hiding. Or at least hidden who and what they really were. Greedy lackeys who couldn't think for themselves.

At least that's what this crew was.

I won't ask you again. Where's your human whore, you weak piece of shit? The largest of the intruders paced back and forth behind his muscle.

You're the one hiding behind those weaker than you. Why don't you come over here and get a taste of how real wolves battle? Aleksei wouldn't normally talk shit like this. He preferred simply to rip out the throats of this kind of trash. Back in the days when he was the best of the Troika Enforcers, he would have already been spitting out their blood.

His months of moping and feeling sorry for himself, of grieving the loss of his alpha, hadn't been good for his fighting skills or his muscle tone. He was out of shape and had it not been for the grey wolf, he and Helena might already be dead, or worse.

Because he wasn't in top form, he was forced to stall for time, to allow Helena to call in the real reinforcements.

The two enforcers lowered their heads, readying for another attack. Even though they'd already gotten their asses beaten down by the grey wolf, they were wearing him down, and they knew it. Aleksei and his new ally, the lone wolf, were all that stood between these bastards and Helena.

What do you want with my...woman? Can't find one of your own? He'd almost fucked up and called Helena his mate. He hadn't marked or claimed her yet. Not officially anyway. He had with his heart and soul, but that didn't outwardly show.

The leader of the mangy crew snarled. *She is of no consequence to me, but she offended the sensibilities of someone much higher up the food chain. I suspect your woman will likely be eaten for lunch to make an example of her. You'd do well to hand her over so you don't end up as collateral damage.*

The grey wolf didn't like that one bit. His hackles rose up and he stood taller. He had the bearing of an alpha who expected the rest of the world to bow down to him.

Just who was this guy?

Aleksei had never seen a wolf fight like this loner before. He was all skill and brutal grace. The closest he'd ever seen to this style of fighting was Niko after he'd come home from Russia. They sure could use Niko's help now. Fuck, he hoped they were on their way.

Because there was no way in hell he was retreating back

into the house where his precious but badass Helena would try to defend them all with nothing more than a piece of wood.

He should have fucking marked her. Maybe then she'd develop the ability to shift, like Galyna had. She was one ferocious wolftress.

Their lovemaking had triggered something in Helena, if she was having visions like Heli and Zara. He'd have to talk to Kosta or Niko about that. Human mates were still new in the wolf world, so nobody yet knew completely how a bite would affect them. Psychic visions and shifting abilities had popped up in most every human, but not until after they'd been marked.

His Helena was special.

Or she'd been marked by another wolf.

No. Couldn't be. He would know. He would have seen her mark. He'd licked every inch of her and hadn't seen anything resembling one. Although Zara had hidden her mark from the world for almost a decade, now that he thought about it. She hadn't even known she'd been marked and was having psychic visions of Niko the whole time.

Fuck. Was that why Helena had a vision of this grey wolf?

Aleksei hadn't known her for very long, and certainly never asked her if she'd had a vision like that before. He stole a glance at the interloper. The guy hadn't even tried to mindspeak with him, just took up sides against the one-bloods. Or maybe it wasn't against them, as much as it was for Helena.

For now Aleksei would take all the help he could get to keep Helena safe. But once he was sure the one-bloods weren't going to get their hands on her, he'd be having a heart to heart with this grey wolf.

If Helena was destined to be another wolf's mate, Aleksei wasn't sure his already fragile heart would survive. If she was his true mate, as he was sure she must be, and this grey wolf thought he could challenge Aleksei for her, he was dead wrong.

He would have to think about that later. The one-bloods were circling, and he had to come up with more ways to stall them.

Aleksei stalked toward the shitheads, doing his best to let them know he wasn't intimidated by them. *Haven't you heard? There's a new Wolf Tzar in town. You're the ones who'd do well to mind your manners. Tzar Nikolai Troika doesn't stand for one-blood antics.*

The grey wolf whipped his head around and stared at Aleksei like he'd said the moon was made of cheese. His eyes glowed with an eerie empty nothingness Even his fur seemed to glow in the moonless night.

The one-bloods all looked at each other as if sharing a secret. For the first time, the leader stepped in front of his enforcers and looked Aleksei straight in the eye. *Oh, we aren't one-bloods. We simply don't recognize your precious Troika's claim to the throne.*

Like you're a better choice to lead Wolfkind into the future?

Not me. But we know who will. Someone your so-called Tzar tried to destroy with his greed for power. He has no idea what kind of enemies he's made. But you go on following your fool if you want. We know better.

That was more than Aleksei could handle. Insult him all they wanted to, but he knew to his very core that Niko was the best of them all and would lead them into a life they deserved. He'd lead even traitors screaming and kicking into a better world, because Tzar Nikolai Troika was a leader for all, not just his own admirers. That's what made him the one true leader of Wolfkind.

Whoever these dumbasses had decided to follow would never be anything but an egotist.

Enough was enough. He lunged at the closest wolf and let his fury loose. Fury for thinking they could come into Troika territory and harm his mate. Fury that they thought they were better than anyone else. And fury for spreading hatred when he'd only just found love.

He plowed into the closest wolf and shoved him to the ground, holding his throat to the dirt. The other wolf flailed and snarled trying to get away, but Aleksei was too strong. *Yield and give your fealty to Tzar Nikolai Troika.*

Never. I'd rather die. The wolf snapped his jaws and tried to scratch at Aleksei's legs, but couldn't get a good angle.

That can be arranged.

Aleksei was ready to snap this miscreant into pieces like the rat that he was. But he wasn't an enforcer anymore and it wasn't his place. Tonight would be the last night that was true. Tomorrow he would go to Max and ask both his forgiveness and for his old job back. Until then, he needed this wolf out of commission.

Now would be a good time for Helena's baseball bat.

The grey wolf bounded into the fray somewhat renewed. He grabbed the big leader with his jaw and tossed him into the side of the house. The window shattered and the boards creaked and splintered with the force.

Good idea. Aleksei used his powerful back legs to donkey

kick the downed enforcer into the wall and on top of the leader. The entire wall of Helena's bedroom caved in an explosion of sparks and flickering of power. The lights in all the nearby houses went dark one by one. They must have hit a power box somewhere. Oops.

That left only the final enforcer to deal with. It circled his fallen comrade, not caring that Aleksei and the grey wolf had taken out his friends. It snarled and looked for a weak spot.

Aleksei's current soft spot came in the form of Helena, dressed only in his t-shirt with her damn bat in one hand, some kind of tiny dagger in the other, and a look of surprise on her face.

"What the fuck did you do to my house?" She held her arms and weapons aloft and gaped at the carnage. "And who do I need to murder?"

The world around him went into slow motion. The two wolves that had been slumped against the rubble of the wall crawled to their feet and turned toward Helena, only a few feet away. The third enforcer crouched, his body angled directly toward her too. The three were going to attack her and there was no way Aleksei would get to her in time.

Sirens sounded from not too far away, probably spurred by the power outage, or maybe the neighbors freaking out at the horror show in the side yard. Luckily, most of the first responder teams in Rogue had at least one Troika, which meant backup was on the way. That gave Aleksei the burst of energy he needed.

Time caught back up with him and Aleksei leapt through the air to put himself in the way of the attack. In an instant he felt only the sting of teeth and claws sinking into his fur and flesh. He fell under the onslaught of the strike, taking blows to his back, ribs, and skull.

He heard Helena scream, but he couldn't quite understand what she was saying. Probably swearing like a sailor if he knew her. She'd be cussing these bastards out like there was no tomorrow. And there might not be for him. He blinked the blood out of his eyes and kicked at the nearest wolf. He couldn't give up yet. He had to make sure Helena was safe first.

Helena. Run.

He got no response. She must not be able to hear him in her head yet. But the grey wolf could. Goddess, he hoped this wasn't a huge mistake. But if Helena had a connection to this wolf, it was his only hope.

Despite his wounds, Aleksei pushed to his feet, lowered his head, and snarled at the leader who was only barely standing himself. He was once again going to try to buy time for either reinforcements or for the grey wolf to help Helena escape.

You'd better be prepared to kill me, because that's the only way you're getting to my mate. But I warn you now, if I go down, you're coming with me. Are you ready to sacrifice your life for your so-called new Tzar?

He didn't give them a chance to answer. He attacked the leader, going directly for the injured back legs. As he ran forward, he called to the grey wolf. *Save the woman. Take her to the Troikas. I swear on my honor, they will not harm you if you assist me in my final hour. Go. Now.*

Aleksei took out the leader, but only momentarily. The other wolves were on him in less than a painful breath, tearing him away. He didn't care, as long as Helena and the grey wolf got away.

He looked to where they last stood and caught only a glimpse of the grey wolf bullying Helena out into the yard with a growl. Good. She probably wouldn't leave him otherwise.

Thank you, brother. He received no reply in the usual mindspeak way, but rather in some strange sense that sent a shiver through his body. It was as if Max or Niko had used their alpha voice on him demanding that he not give up. It was a demand he could not ignore. He must obey. To his last breath he would fight for his life.

A soft, but strong feminine voice filtered into his head. *Not for your life, but for your love.*

NOT SO BIG BAD WOLVES

The wolf nipped at her heels, hurrying her through the woods. God, she hoped her gut was right and it wasn't taking her to its den to kill and eat her. This was why no one was allowed in the Reserve after dark. Wolves. Or rather werewolves, as she'd learned recently. Some of her best friends were werewolves, as it turned out. Not this guy though. She wasn't even a hundred percent sure he was a shifter. So far he hadn't shown any signs of humanity whatsoever. "Don't be so pushy, I'm going as fast as I can."

Thank God for all those pole classes she taught. Hanging upside down on a metal pole in front of horny people was easy. Jogging was so not her thing. She already had a stitch in her side and if she stepped on one more unidentified squishy thing with her bare feet she might give up.

No. She could never do that. Aleksei needed her help. She could only pray that this wolf knew that and was on her side.

Her next step wasn't something soft or even slimy. A rock or a pile of razor blades bit into the ball of her foot.

"Ow, ow. God dammit. Someone needs to come in here and pave some better walking paths."

The wolf replied by sniffing her foot and giving it a little yippy bark. Then it shoved her leg with its snout and forced her to keep going. Asshole.

"Please tell me we're close to wherever we're going and that there will be help there." This random jaunt through the woods wasn't doing any good if he wasn't taking her to get help. Helplessness was not a feeling she was used to. Helena rubbed her arms and took a tentative step forward. She was going to need a month's worth of pedicures and foot rubs if she lived through the night.

The wolf gave her another shove forward and then lowered its head and growled. Helena stumbled and barely stopped herself from falling. "What the hell? What are you growling at? You'd better not be putting me in danger or I'll have to skin you and use you for a rug later."

He ignored her completely and growled deeper. The hair on his back actually stood up in spikey tufts, exactly like in the movies. Shit. Something bad was about to go down. It crept forward and nipped at her ankles, making her jump forward again.

A rustling sounded from all sides but mainly directly in front of her. The grey wolf made a weird barking sound and then took off running the opposite direction. Before Helena could even start to follow it, she was surrounded by a whole new group of enormous wolves. The sensation of the fine hairs on her arms and the back of her neck had her sucking in a breath that she couldn't seem to release. That bastard grey wolf had led her straight into a trap.

These ones weren't mangy like the others. Great. At least

she was going to be eaten alive by a pack who cleaned up after themselves.

Two more tore past her, hot on the grey wolf's trail. She was on her own for real this time.

"Nice wolfy, wolfies. Don't eat me. I'm not delicious at all." Except according to Aleksei, who was in danger. If she didn't get herself out of this situation, she wouldn't be able to help him. Fuck that.

The closest wolf's head was almost at her eye level and she smacked him on the nose. "Bad dog. Sit."

That shocked the hell out of him. He did in fact sit down, tipped his head to the side, and looked at her like 'what the hell, lady?'

"Good boy. Now take me to your leader." Geez. She sounded ridiculous.

The wolf she'd smacked coughed - or maybe it was laughing? Okay, so it could understand. Because they'd come at her so snarly, she assumed these were part of Team Bad Guy, but this was going to be extra embarrassing if they turned out to be wolf-shifters she knew in real life.

She looked into the eyes of the laughing wolf to see if she recognized anything. The only thing really familiar was the same blue glow that Aleksei had. Did this mean they were in his pack? She really should have had that talk with Heli about hooking up with a Troika. Someone really needed to write *The Girl's Guide to Supernatural Dating*.

That was going on her to do list. Just as soon as she saved her lover, took out the bad guys, and finally got to eat her Thanksgiving leftovers.

The wolf in front of her continued to laugh, but also bowed its head and Helena heard the sickening sound of bones cracking and watched the fur split across its back. Gross.

In a blink or two the laughing wolf became a stark-naked man. Eek. It was the bartender from Sleepy Folk. Crap, what was his name? She was completely distracted by all that man flesh and could not think of his name, and she totally knew it, she really really did. This had to be what dudes at the club felt like when she took all of her clothes off.

"Helena? What are you doing in the Reserve?"

She dragged her eyes away from his giant package and made sure not to let them drift any lower than his chin. Now that she had her gawking under control, she finally remembered his name. Harley. Phew. She blurted out, "Aleksei's in trouble."

"Why was that wolf attacking you?" He looked off into the direction the grey wolf and his buddies had run and scowled. "Who is he?"

"What? No? That grey wolf? He was helping me. He brought me to you guys. I think. It's confusing. Who cares, we have to go help Aleksei."

Harley frowned and then looked her up and down like he was just realizing she was running around the woods half-naked. She gave Aleksei's shirt a tug downwards. It was only barely covering her hoo-ha. If the wolves were any smaller, they'd all have seen right up in her business.

"That was a lone wolf. They are very dangerous. Max and Niko are going to want to ask you questions about him. That is, if our Troika Enforcers don't get to him first." He waved Helena forward and the other two wolves flanked the two of them.

Great, she was being herded again like a fucking sheep.

119

"Harley, you aren't listening. I don't give a flying foot fuck about the grey wolf or whether he's alone or not. You have to come with me back to my house, right now."

"The pack house is just up ahead. Selena will have clothes for you and a place to clean up. The alphas and their mates are already there and will explain—"

"Are you shitting me? Kosta, Heli, and the others are all here? Come on, hurry up. We gotta go round everybody up and bring reinforcements back to my place." She smacked him on the arm and jogged on ignoring the pain in her feet, her side, and her heart.

Selena Troika, dressed as if she was hosting a board meeting for some fancy pants corporation, waited for her at the big French doors at the back of the house. She had a plush spa-style full-length robe held out and a pair of soft slippers at her feet.

Helena didn't realize just how cold she was or how dirty her legs and feet were until she slipped into the comforting material. "Thank you, but I'm hoping you have some leggings and, I don't know, like a flack jacket I can borrow too."

"Don't worry dear, we'll take care of you now."

"Selena, please. I don't need to be taken care of. We have to get Aleksei some backup. He's fighting some really ugly, mean wolves and I think he's in a lot of trouble." She didn't want to say how she was worried it was a whole lot more than just trouble. She refused to believe he was...nope. Not even gonna think that.

"Helena, come in. Your Aleksei is indeed in trouble, but he's alive and we will do everything we can to get him back."

Selena waved her into the house as calm as can be, but Helena heard the worry in her voice.

"What do you mean get him back? You know something, spill. He's important to me." More than that, but she had to keep her emotions in check, because her imagination was already spiraling down, down, down into the depths, wondering what would she do without him.

"I know he is. Well, I mean I knew he would be. You're true mates. I wasn't sure either of you would allow the connection to happen, especially not this fast. I'm glad you have. It may be what saves him." She led Helena through a formal living room. The deep male voices of her boss, and his brothers came from nearby.

There were far too many questions and not enough time. Helena wanted to ask Selena about the knowing they were true mates thing, but finding out what she knew about Aleksei had to take priority. "What's going on in there? Do they know what's happened to Aleksei? Can they help?"

Selena stopped in front of a bathroom with a hot shower already running, a stack of clothes on the counter, and every beauty product she might ever need, including some healing balm for her feet. She took Helena by the shoulders and squeezed. "Take a minute to take care of yourself. We can't do anything for Aleksei running around like chickens with our heads flapping around and bloody. Once you're cleaned up, we'll figure out how to rescue your mate. Okay?"

Her mate. She didn't entirely understand what that meant, but she knew it felt right. "Okay. I won't be more than a few minutes. Tell those boys of yours to be ready to kick some ass."

When Helena was showered and dressed in the clothes

that somehow fit perfectly, were functional and flattering all at the same time, she hurried to the dining room. Heli jumped up out of her chair and grabbed her in a long, hard bear hug. "We're here for you, okay?"

The second Heli let go, she picked up a plate full of cookies and shoved them toward Helena.

Uh-oh. This was bad. If Heli was stress baking, some serious shit was going down. Helena took a cookie and used it as her weapon of choice. "You tell me everything I need to know right now, or I will dunk this cookie in orange juice and put it down the garbage disposal."

"Huaah." Heli gasped and was strangled by the threat at the same time, so it came out all garbled. Kosta came to her rescue and snatched the cookie from Helena's hand, shoving it into his mouth.

He made mean squinty eyes at Helena, but she gave them right back. "Look. I know I'm not up to speed on this whole wolf pack war thing, or the details of being a mate, or whatever. But Aleksei is mine now, and if you don't tell me what's going on, what the plan is to fix it, and like a dozen other things, I'm marching right out the door, calling every single one of the girls at the club, and we are going to solve this problem ourselves. Don't you dare tell me a band of exotic dancers can't, because we deal with sleazeballs and dumbasses every day, and there isn't a woman among us that won't cut a bitch if we have to."

Kosta looked at Max and Niko, smirked, and said, "Told ya."

Niko shook his head. "We are not ready to reveal ourselves to the whole damn world yet. I will not put every wolf at risk because someone wants to usurp my title. Fuck it. Let them. See if they can do better."

Zara rubbed her hand up and down Niko's arm. "No one is a better man to lead the wolves than you are, sweetheart."

Niko looked up at the ceiling and sighed. Uneasy is the head that wears a crown. Helena wanted to feel for Niko, but it wasn't getting her the answers she needed or the actions to help Aleksei. "So...am I walking out of here to get my girl gang, or are you puppy dogs going to do something besides sit around and sniff each other's butts?"

Galyna raised her hand. "I volunteer to be on the girl gang. I've been trying to tell these guys for months that the people of Rogue can handle this, but somebody had to go and have visions of dragons coming to town or some such ridiculous thing and now we're sitting on our bums. I say, girl power for the win."

Dragons? Was that a thing? Like, for real, like werewolves? And that was not something she was ever going to say out loud. She blurted out, "Hey, I had a vision too and mine said let's quit yapping and get to saving the world."

The whole room looked at her like she'd said boo to a baby. Selena grinned with an I-told-you-so gleam, but everyone else was clearly shocked. "You can all close your jaws and tell me what me having a vision means later. Let's. Go."

She waved them toward the back door, but instead of them going out, a pack of wolves came bounding in. But none of them was Aleksei.

Harley shifted into his naked self again right in front of the whole room. One would think with her job she wouldn't care who was naked and who wasn't, but she did. Maybe because while Harley had the goods to make some woman very, very happy, he was still no Aleksei.

"Sir," he addressed Max who nodded that he should continue. "We lost the grey wolf. He's like a fucking ghost or something. Just disappeared. No trail. not even a fucking scent to follow."

They all looked at Helena. "What? It's not like I'm friends with any other wolves besides you guys. That's about all the supernatural friends I can handle at the moment. He helped me and Aleksei, and he was in my vision. I'm pretty sure he's one of the good guys, but you all are so damn secretive, what do I know?"

Zara studied her for a moment longer than everyone else. "We should talk about your vision later. I'd like to know the interval between when Aleksei marked you and they started."

"I don't know what marked me means." While they were fooling around Aleksei had said something about wanting to mark her, but then they'd gotten to the good parts and she'd forgotten all about it. Must be some wolf thing. She hoped it didn't mean he had to pee on her or something. Like marking his territory. Gross.

"You know, when he bit you and you got your—" Heli pulled the collar of her t-shirt aside. A tattoo of a purple full moon with a howling wolf in the center practically glowed on her collarbone.

Lots of women in her profession were covered in tattoos. Helena had never found a design she wanted to have on her skin for the rest of her life. But holy wow, a butterfly or a heart or even a skull and crossbones had nothing on the beauty of the wolf on Heli. Helena was a bit jealous. "I don't have anything like that."

Heli frowned. "Are you sure?"

"I'm ninety percent naked for the majority of my days. I'm pretty sure I would have noticed if someone had painted a glowing tattoo on me."

Selena poured herself a cup of tea and held it up to Helena in cheers sort of gesture. "Sometimes the soul marks its mate before the body has a chance to. I know of one other wolftress who developed powers after meeting her true mate, even though she was never marked by him. That's the power of love."

The rest of the room sat stunned by what Selena said, but Helena felt buoyed by her words. She did love Aleksei, and he loved her. And now she was done talking and was going to go save her mate.

Helena nodded toward Gal, indicating she could come along, and walked toward the front door of the house this time. Screw walking through the woods. She was borrowing aka stealing someone's car, going to the club to get her girls, and going on the hunt.

"Wait," Harley said. "Uh, you shouldn't leave yet."

"I've had enough of you boys standing around holding your enormous dicks. I've got a mate to go save, with or without your help." She came here thinking the Troikas were her only hope. Seemed like politics was going to get in the way. She never cared for politics.

"But we got more information on Aleksei. We found out before you got here that he'd been taken and was being held by this new faction."

"Great. Then let's go take them out."

"I mean. We can and we probably should. But it's Max's place to declare war on them since he's the alpha who can demand blood for blood, a life for a life."

Max swore not quite under his breath. "Fuck."

Blood for blood. A life for a life.

The trembles from before came back, but this time they rattled all the way to her bones. Her vision didn't go dark, and she didn't see a grey wolf or anything else, but everything just went blurry and she had to get control of her hands to wipe the tears out of her eyes.

"No. Don't say it. Don't. It's not true, you don't know what you're talking about. I would know. I would know."

The women surrounded her in a giant group hug, which almost insulated her from hearing Harley's next words. Almost.

"Aleksei's dead. Killed by this wolf who wants to be the new Tzar."

NOT NOT DEAD

*W*as he dead?

Sure as hell felt like he was. Every bone in his human body had cracks in them. All two hundred and six. Maybe that's why he couldn't seem to shift into his wolf form. Two-hundred-ish was a whole lot less to heal that the three-hundred-ish of his wolf. But damn, he was sure as shit missing his fur right now, and his ability to see better in the dark.

There wasn't a single twinkle of light in this cold place. Fuck. Maybe he was dead and this was purgatory.

Didn't all dogs go to heaven?

If this was the good place, shouldn't there be fluffy clouds, rainbows, lots of rare steaks, and pumpkin pie with whipped cream smothered all over angels? His angel would look and taste and smell like his mate.

Helena, Helena, Helena. The ache in his bones receded, the chill across his skin faded, but still his wolf remained silent, even when her name was on his lips.

Fuck. Where was Helena? That grey wolf better have gotten her safely away, or Aleksei was going to haunt his ass from here to eternity.

While he was pretty sure his eyes were open, everything from the inside out felt...wrong. He didn't know which way was up, down, or if he way lying down, or suspended in the air.

"It's a very strange feeling, isn't it? Not having access to your wolf. Might as well be dead." A female voice that could have been death itself reverberated around in his head as if his mind was a cold, stone cave.

Aleksei licked his lips, trying to find his voice through the desert of his mouth and sore throat. He managed to croak out a few words. "Who are you?"

"Was I so insignificant to you Troikas you don't even remember me?" She didn't exactly sound hurt. Was this woman friend or foe?

"It's been a shitty day, lady. All I want to know is if we're friends or enemies." And if she could help him get out of here and back to Helena, that would be great. Or off on his mission to kill the grey wolf if he needed to, now that he knew he wasn't dead.

But what was that she'd said about not having access to his wolf?

"A long time ago, we were allies. But then Nikolai fucked up the world, my father fucked it up some more, and I lost everything. So I think at best we're frenemies, Troika."

"Taryn?" If he'd guessed right, this was the daughter of the defunct Crescent Bay pack. Her father had murdered Piotr Troika. Stabbed him in the back when the Troikas had come to the Crescents seeking an alliance by mating her to one of the Troika sons.

Aleksei had been on that mission. The one that destroyed his world. It had cost him his alpha, his sanity, and almost his life. His only joy in the last year was hearing that Niko had defeated Taryn's father in a battle to the death and claimed the pack as was his right.

Taryn had disappeared that day and hadn't been seen since. What was she doing here in whatever dark prison they were in?

"Ah, so you do remember me. Well, at least someone does." Her voice got quieter until it was almost a whisper. "Not that it matters now. Neither you nor I will ever see the light of the moon ever again."

Of anyone, Aleksei understood exactly where Taryn was coming from. All up in her head, letting the darkness of depression consume her. Been there, done that, got the scars. Only he'd been lucky. His pack hadn't allowed him to wither away to the nothingness that Taryn had become. Selena had brought him back into the light where he'd found the one person that could make his soul burn with life again.

He would not die here in the darkness. Not as long as his Helena was out there somewhere waiting for him. "Taryn, we are getting out of here. You hear me?"

She laughed in that way people who have given up do. Sad, joyless, almost-sobs came from her. "No, we aren't. He needs us too much to ever let us go. We can't defeat him. You should learn that now. It's better to join him."

What the fuck?

"Join who? What are you talking about? This sounds like

some bullshit. You're a wolftress. Get your shit together and let's find a way to get out of here." Never in his life had he known a wolf to back down from any fight. Even the stinking one-bloods fought for what they believed in, even as crazy as those beliefs were. This attitude of joining the dark side just because it was too hard or it hurt too much to do what was right, that simply wasn't the wolf way.

"I'm no longer a wolftress, and you aren't a wolf. You'll see, Troika. You'll see." She was almost angry in her despair.

Aleksei gentled his tone. If Taryn had been captured by this new faction that wanted to take down Niko as the Wolf Tzar and had kept her here, making her think she was no longer a wolf, they'd done a lot of damage to a woman who was once a savvy and powerful wolftress. "Of course we are. We were born shifters. No one but the Goddess can take that away."

"Try to shift, try to even feel your wolf, then tell me you're still a child of the Moon Goddess." Taryn spat out the words.

He closed his eyes to focus, and called on his wolf. All he found deep in his soul where the wolf lived was more darkness, total emptiness. He shuddered.

"It's not there, is it?"

What had they done to him, to her? "Who? How? Why?"

Aleksei could hardly get those questions out. All he could think about was this hollow place inside.

"The demon wolf."

Umm. No. That wasn't a thing, and her saying something so crazy made his instincts flare back to life. No way he'd lost his own wolf, it was perhaps suppressed but he'd never believe it wasn't there at all. So, think. What was really going on here?

Niko had defeated an incubus who'd allied itself with some kind of demon dragon. They'd used the wolves as pawns in their own war. But when Niko became the Wolf Tzar, he'd extricated all of wolfkind from that game. That was the only demon Aleksei had ever heard of interfering with other supernaturals. Those kinds of creatures usually kept to themselves.

Except Taryn had grown up in Crescent Bay, or Cape Cod as it was known in the human world. It was well known that the King of the Incubus, Leon, had a home there with his demon family. The wolves had never had any trouble with any Incubus or Succubus. Why would they want to get involved in the aftermath of the pack war? That couldn't be it. Yet she'd called him a demon wolf.

"He's our master now." Taryn sounded a bit maniacal now, and Aleksei was worried about how long she'd been here in the dark and if she'd developed some kind of Stockholm syndrome for this so-called demon wolf. "He's taken the power of your wolf and mine, and he wants more."

Aleksei let the splices of information roll around in his mind. The Incubus demon Niko had defeated posed as a Volkov. Every wolf on the planet bowed to the Volkovs' ancient power. The oldest among them, Rasputin, struck a deal with the devil to be practically immortal. Yes, this demon wolf had Rasputin written all over him.

There were not enough swear words in English or Russian to express the severity of their situation if Rasputin was behind the new faction of wolves and their imprisonment. He'd already brought down one Wolf Tzar for shits and giggles. He'd be much more dangerous if he was actually trying.

But Aleksei was making a lot of assumptions here, with only a wolftress under extreme duress for information. The only solution he could see to this problem was to figure out how to get the fuck out of this cage of darkness. So far that had proven impossible to even comprehend, much less strategize.

He sure as shit could use a good dose of Helena's kickass, take-no-prisoners sassy attitude right now. Since he didn't have her in person, he imagined the sweet scent and taste of her, pictured the way she grinned at him like they had a secret no one else knew, and clung to the soul-deep sense that the two of them belonged together.

What would Helena do?

She was all about the girl power. Possibly for the first time ever, Aleksei wished he had a vagina. Since it was unlikely he was going to grow one in the next few minutes, he had to go with what he did have. At the moment that was a pile of broken bones, a gaping chasm of darkness, a semi-carazy wolftress, and a whole lot of guesses as to who his enemy was and why he'd been captured instead of killed.

In other words, diddly squat.

He was fucked.

Aleksei wanted very much to live so that he could spend the rest of his life loving Helena. He'd fought hard not to believe this was it. But unless something pretty fucking huge changed, or someone came to rescue his ass, there was no way he could make that happen.

Floating here in the darkness, blacker than the night both in his soul and all around him, Aleksei retreated back to the place he'd exiled himself to, before he'd met Helena. The cold embrace of defeat wrapped its arms around him once more. He'd known it before and if he let it take over again, it would insulate his mind in a numbness that would protect the tiniest flicker of hope.

He closed his eyes, not because it blocked out any light, but from sheer exhaustion. Mentally, physically, to his soul, his energy was gone. It was too easy to slip into the oblivion without his wolf inside to spur him on. On one last long breath, Aleksei gave up.

The room stayed eerily quiet for a thousand years while he floated in pain and despair.

Or maybe it was only a thousand seconds.

Taryn's voice broke through the darkness. "Ah, there it is. That's what I've been waiting for."

He almost asked what she meant, what she wanted, but he simply didn't care.

"You've given up. It took you longer than the other wolves under my rule, but it didn't take as long as I thought it would for an all-powerful Troika." A spark of ugly black magic filtered into the room and wrapped itself around Aleksei's soul.

Under her rule. Not a demon, not Rasputin. Taryn Crescent, the one who'd lost everything.

His new mistress. The one to rule wolfkind. The one to have her revenge.

"I knew you were the right choice. Although you almost slipped through my fingers when that meddling wolftress found you a mate. That's okay. It makes your wolf all the stronger for having experienced a taste of what it can never feel again. You'll be the perfect vessel to bring my consort out of the underworld."

Yes, her consort.

Taryn's...

Consort...

From the Underworld....

That didn't make any sense. Aleksei scraped and clawed his way back to consciousness, back to caring about what happened. He would be no other woman's consort. He and his soul belonged to Helena, and her alone.

He opened his eyes, and this time saw the light of fire and lava. Heat replaced the chill around his heart. The voice of Taryn receded and became something as old as death itself. He stared into the eyes, not of the wolftress he knew, but of a crone, a black witch.

"What have you done with Taryn?"

"She is of no consequence to you anymore."

Taryn was of no consequence to him anymore. The cares he had about her...and another woman that he couldn't quite bring to mind, even though he somehow knew she was important, all melted away like his brain was nothing more than liquified Jell-O.

"Yes, that's right. Let go of it all. Make room for his chaos to come in. He will so enjoy running wild as your wolf."

Yes, chaos. His soul was already in turmoil. Where was the calming peace he'd found?

Gone. Gone. Gone.

Two words filtered through his mind as a great force, turbulent and strong, crushed its way into his body, taking over his heart, mind, and soul.

Zhin moya. My life.

He wasn't begging for his own existence. His plea to the universe, or the Goddess, or whoever might listen and hear his cry, was only to be soothed by his mate once again.

But she was lost to him. They could never be together ever again.

AMAZEBALLS CHANGE THE WORLD

*N*ooooooope.

No way, no how. Aleksei was not dead. Helena didn't know how she knew, but she was one-thousand million trillion kabillion percent sure.

And just for making her doubt it for a half second, she punched Harley square on the jaw. Boom. "Don't ever say anything like that ever again, asshole, or I'll knock your block off."

Harley cupped his jaw and opened and closed his mouth a few times. "Are you sure you aren't at least part wolf? That's one hell of a right hook you've got."

"Don't make me come at you again." She held up her other hand and made the come-at-me finger motion.

Harley grinned, like he had mad respect for her going all Uma Thurman in Kill Bill on his ass. The Troikas were weird, and she liked it.

Niko held up a hand between them. "Harley, maybe you'd better tell us where you got this intel.

"From me." A pretty young woman walked into the

dining room, but she was only vaguely familiar to Helena. She lived in town, but Helena couldn't remember the last time she'd seen her anywhere.

"Key?" Galyna ran to the girl's side and guided her over to a seat at the table next to Selena, like she was someone fragile.

Helena thought she saw Key make a resigned face and roll her eyes, but if she had it was fleeting. Then she was all seriousness. She sat and folded her hands in her lap. Her eyes went all eerie and white and she breathed in several long, deep breaths, as if meditating or something.

Helena wanted to shout that this wasn't the time to Namaste, but she held her tongue. If Key was having a vision anything like what she'd had, there was no controlling it. Patience was not her virtue, but understanding was.

Key blinked a few times and her own eye colored returned. With a shaky hand, She took a cup of tea Selena offered her. "Thank you."

After a few sips, Helena was holding tight to her last nerve. Pretty soon she was going to smack the pretty china teacup across the room. Heli glanced at Key, then at Helena, grabbed the cup from Key and set it on the opposite side of the table. "I like that tea set. Don't go breaking it."

How did she know?

Zara nodded at Helena like she knew what was in her head too. "Some kind of psychic abilities like Heli's, mine, Key's, and now yours, are common when a human is marked or mated to a wolf. I swear I'm going to write a Girl's Guide to Supernatural Dating or something that we can hand out when new mates come along.

Hey. That was her idea. Maybe Zara's power was pulling

thoughts out of other people's head. Whatever, they'd co-write it and make a million dollars each. Key must be mated to a wolf too. They could all write a chapter. Later.

Key looked up at Helena. "Sorry. I just wanted to make sure of what I saw."

Finally, let's get on with it. "What did you see?"

"I had one of those visions, you know, like a lion, a witch, and a wardrobe walk into a bar kind of deal. I'm working on trying to remember them better and I can call bits of them up now, but every time I do, I fritz out the nearest electronic device. Today it just happened to be my freaking cell phone. Again. Sorry, I would have just called otherwise."

Helena folded her arms and made the go-on hand swirl at her. She wasn't going to trust what Key thought she saw if she tried to say Aleksei was dead.

"Aleksei is...well, he's not dead. But he's not not-dead either. I think. I don't totally understand what I'm seeing. There is a woman with him too and she's in the same state. He called her Taryn. Does anyone know who that is?"

Zara and Niko exchanged knowing looks at each other. Niko voiced what they were thinking. "Taryn Crescent. We've been looking for her since I defeated her father in an alpha challenge and we took over the pack. She was the rightful heir."

"Let's save the pack politics lesson for later and hear what else Key can tell us. Helena is likely to start smashing faces and dishes if we don't get on with it, I'm afraid." Heli indicated for Key to go on.

That's what best friends were for.

"Well, I ran right over to Sleepy Folk to tell somebody what I'd seen, but they said you all were here. And then I heard the sirens and stuff and, well, you know how I feel about the Sheriff's department."

"Yeah. That you have a crush on the Sheriff Reagan McHotsalot," Heli interjected.

Key turned about fourteen shades of pink. "Umm, so I headed over there to see if someone could get you guys on the radio. Apparently there was some kind of house explosion...?"

Helena groaned. "If by explosion you mean WWE were-wolf edition, that's my house. Dammit."

"Ooh. Sorry. I think you're going to need another place to stay for a while." Key grimaced. "Anyway, I told your guy what I saw, he called whoever, and I gather thanks to the game of telephone whispers all you heard was the Aleksei's dead part."

"I don't really care that much about the house. I want to know where Aleksei and this Taryn woman are. I've been telling you all for a half an hour, he needs backup, and now we have to go save his ass. Man, having a fake werewolf boyfriend is so much work."

"Fake?" Key asked.

"Long story. Anyway, he's mine now and I'm keeping him. Tell us where to find them." For being wolves and shit, these Troikas were the settin'-around-est bunch of old fogies she'd ever met.

Key shrugged her shoulders. "I dunno know. That's all I got."

Baby Jesus Christ on a cracker. She was going to have to solve this problem herself, just like she did every other damn thing in her life. Except this time she didn't have a chance in hell. Her knowledge of supernatural stuff was spotty at best.

She was about to turn and walk right out of that dining room, when Heli grabbed her by the wrist.

"Don't go. You don't have to do anything alone anymore. I know that's your natural response, to take charge and just do everything yourself, but you've got so many people you can ask to help you. You're the one to pull us all together, you're the linchpin, but even the strongest pin still needs a wheel to go anywhere."

Whoa. "Is this one of your psychic moments?"

"Nope. This is me being your friend and telling you not to put your head in your butt if you want to really go after and get what you want."

Gulp. Helena hadn't seen that coming. Okay. Geez. She could take a hint. If she was the linchpin, she needed a wheel. With a lot of spokes. She looked around the circle of women and that's where inspiration struck.

"Hey, Kosta, who else at the club is dating a wolf and maybe doesn't know it yet?"

His eyes went wide, but Heli raised her eyebrows like she saw where Helena was going with this. "We're about to out a bunch of the pack, aren't we? It's about frickin' time. I told you, honey."

Kosta rolled his eyes, but Zara and Galyna were giving similar looks of told-you-so to Max and Niko. Max shook his head, in that way that meant he didn't agree but was doing whatever Gal wanted him to do. Niko frowned and growled.

Zara winked at Helena and sat in Niko's lap. "Now, sweetheart. You've known this was coming for a while. I warned you. Don't get all Tzary on us now. This is the right thing to do even if you aren't ready for it."

Niko's eyes glowed a brilliant amber gold looking at his Queen...or rather Tzarina. "Not all humans are as open-minded as you are, *solnyshkaya*. Nor are they as good at keeping secrets. We aren't ready for the whole world to know."

"No, but we can start with our small part of the world and build from there. Starting with the girls at the Naughty Wolf, oh and that one bouncer."

The glow in Niko's eyes faded back to his normal bright whites and he nodded.

Heli clapped and jumped up. "Okay, let's call Lanette, Linda, Daphine, Frania, Debbie, Corinne, Susie, Sharon, Danielle, Carrie, Debra, Nicole, Christine, Alida, Jennifer, Angela, Mari, Deonne, Celia, Jennifer, Courtney, Barb, Rosita, Bobbie," she took a deep breath, "Andrea, Judy, Natalie, Melissa, Connie, Aracelis, Kat, Ally, Shirley, Rebecca, Alicia, Amanda, Betsy, Stephanie, Carina, Katherine, Carol, Christine, Brenda, Liz, Ann, Karen, Larelle, Tracey, Lisa," she just kept ticking names off of her fingers, "Tamye, Katrena, Nichole, Trina, Kathy, Stacy, Lahudyne, Jessy, Margaret, Jeanette, Alexa, Nita, Lynda, Li, Tamesha, Toni, Sarita, Angie, Kerry, Lisa, Sydney, Michele, Alisa, Michelle, Joyce, Cynthia, Selena, Crystal, Samantha, Lynn, Glenda, Julie, Catherine, Krystyn, Anne, Shiralee, Vi, and," one more giant breath, "Dale."

Helena held up her hand. "All those people don't work at the club, I'm the manager, I would know, and how do you remember all those names?"

Heli shrugged. "No, they don't all work at the club, but they are all intimately involved with wolves, which of course, makes them amazeballs. So I make it my business to know. I probably forgot a few and if I did, I'm sorry. They should email me later and I'll add their name to the printed version."

"I think we're gonna need like a Facebook group or something to get everyone in the loop." Plus a telephone tree or something.

Selena picked up her phone and waved it in the air. "They've all been invited via my secret code to Wolfspace. But I'd suggest we gather the core girls from the club and start to spread the word from there. What is your plan after that?"

Luckily, Helena had gotten a good solid five minutes to think about that while Heli had been listing off pretty much every woman in town. "How many do you think have some kind of psychic powers or something?"

Selena gave a one-shoulder shrug. "Depends on if they're fated mates or not. I'll put a poll in the Wolfspace group to find out."

"Well, let's try to get as many of them together as we can."

Zara tapped her lip. "You're thinking we can pool our powers?"

"I mean...' Helena nodded slowly. I'm making this up as I go, but yeah."

Niko stood and started taking off his clothes. "I think the power of the sacred circle can only help. We'll gather the packs, you gather their significant others and we'll meet there in an hour. The other guys all shed their shirts and pants in a second and shifted into huge wolves.

Helena had officially seen one too many giant peens today. She only cared to ever see one Troika's manly bits for the rest of her life. This plan had better work.

Within half an hour she and Heli had half a dozen women piled into the back of Kosta's purple vintage pick-up. They didn't have to worry about getting pulled over because there was a whole line of police cars in front of and behind them carrying more probable mates. About a third of them had been filled in and indicated they had some kind of ability, psychic or not. The rest were getting told that they'd find out exactly what was what when they got to this sacred area in the Reserve.

As promised, Niko, Max, Kosta, and a whole slew of other wolves were waiting in a beautiful clearing that Helena never even knew existed in this protected piece of forest.

A few dozen wolves shifted and went to greet their girlfriends and boyfriends. There were definitely some shocked faces, but on the whole the humans were simply happy to see their significant others not having to hide who or what they were. More than a few used hands, scarves, coats, and other items or body parts to cover all the nakedness.

Niko and Zara came over to join Helena who was the only unpartnered human. "This is your show. What do you want us to do?"

Helena had taken a lot of dance growing up and one particular one came to mind as right for the occasion. "Wolves around the outside in a circle, women or humans or other people who identify as psychics and mates in the inside circle. You guys go clockwise around us, and we'll do our thing in the middle."

God, she hoped this would work.

The group of humans joined her in the center of the clearing when she waved them over. Niko shifted and howled. The rest of the wolves followed his lead and shifted back into their four-legged furry versions, then took up their places about three feet behind the group gathered in the middle.

"I'm the first to admit, I'm pulling this out of my butt, but there doesn't exactly seem to be a manual for how to be a supernatural mate, so anyone who has an idea, feel free to speak up."

One lady raised her hand. "I started making some notes about being a shifter's girlfriend, sort of a guide. I can bring it next time."

"Yeah. I had that idea too. When this is all over, let's form a book club or something," another girl said and nodded.

"I want everyone to hold hands and we're going to start by just walking in a circle, but I've always believed there is power in dance, so if the music moves you, shake your groove thang. The point is for us to all, I don't know, get on the same wavelength or something. I'm hoping someone will get a vision or whatever that will point us to where Aleksei and Taryn are being held. Then the wolves will take point and mount a rescue."

Writer girl raised her hand again. "What music?"

Well, shit.

Heli grabbed the woman's hand next to her and nodded at everyone else to do the same. Awesome. At least someone was organized. She hoped Heli's phone or bluetooth speaker would be loud enough, and the music was danceable.

A beautiful woman who Helena didn't recognize, dressed all in white, with gorgeous olivy-brown skin and a twinkle in her eye, took Helena's hand, and Zara's with the other.

"Oh, I don't think we've met," Zara said. "Are you a wolf's mate? I'm Zara."

"Oh, we've met, dear. I'm most definitely a shifter's mate. Just here to help and lend my powers. Shall we?" She nodded toward Heli.

Heli wrinkled up her nose and sucked in a deep breath. Then she started singing. "At first I was afraid, I was petrified..."

Helena snorted, but joined in, as did every other woman in the circle. They walked, holding hands, and singing I Will Survive at the top of their lungs. The second they got to the disco drop, every single human started shaking and shimmying and swaying to the beat.

That's when something magical happened.

The wolves howled up at the moon, and the light of its rays intensified right before their eyes. Dozens of beams shot down from the sky and highlighted the dancers as if they were each the star of the show. There were tall women and short ones. Curvy girls with jiggly bits, and medium sized girls with big butts and small butts and in-between butts. There were thin girls with smiles, and skinny girls with tears in their eyes. Every size, shape, skin color, ability, belief, fear, hope, and dream were joined together, as one, and it was magnificent.

The woman in white leaned over to Helena and whispered in her ear. "This is how we change the world. Girl power."

ZHIN MOYA, MY LIFE

*A*leksei had never fought with his own wolf before, but he was now. The beast was trying its best to claw its way back into Aleksei's soul and every time it scratched or bit at his broken human body, Aleksei saw nothing but blood and destruction in the wolf's intention.

This was not his wolf. It had been taken over by something dark and malevolent. Something chaotic.

The wolf attacked him again and again, but even though he tore at skin and bones, without Aleksei's acquiescence he couldn't get back into the soul. The one thing keeping Aleksei fighting and sane was the knowledge that the place inside he'd feared was desolate and empty wasn't. It was filled with the love of Helena.

With each strike, his body grew weaker, but his spirit grew stronger. It was as if she was there with him, filling him with her light.

The wolf charged again and the black witch screeched. A ray of light, bright and piercing in this utter darkness, shone like a beacon. It was more than that, the light became both Aleksei's weapon and his defense.

He pulled on the last reserves of his body and moved toward the little beam. The closer he got to it, the brighter and wider it grew, as if it too was reaching for him.

"No. You must join with him before he reaches the light." The witch screamed, but then turned her back on the bright ray and sank farther into the darkness.

The wolf lunged toward him one last time, its eyes burning with a black fire not unlike that of the grey wolf. The moment it crashed into Aleksei, he reached the beam of moonlight and stood up in its full glorious illumination. The power of the wolf's jump knocked him down, but not out of the ray.

Whatever had been possessing the wolf melted away into the darkness. Aleksei swore he heard the feathers of a large bird, as big as a great owl, swoop, rustle, then fly away.

The wolf lay on top of him, as if dead. Its fur sparkled like polished steel in the moonlight. Slowly its form faded and the magic of its being sank back into Aleksei, joining together with him once again.

Without even realizing he was doing it, Aleksei shifted, welcoming the warmth and healing power of his wolf back home. He lay bathing in the pure beautiful light of the moon which seemed to dance all over him.

"Aleksei? Aleksei! Oh my god. There he is, help me get to him. Hurry." Helena's voice filtered through the haze of his recovering mind and soul. It was like a balm that nothing else could have ever provided.

He tried to get to his feet, but he simply didn't have any strength left. His wolf begged him to be still and let it heal them both a little longer. It was smart enough to know that she would come to his side.

In another breath, she was there. "Oh Aleksei, tell me you're okay. When I saw that horrible witch looking lady doing her impression of the galactic emperor on you, we sent all of the light straight for her. Tell me we did enough. Oh, my Aleksei."

My Aleksei. He liked the sound of that. *I'm here, love. I'm not entirely okay, but I will be now that you've found me. Let's never be apart again.*

She dropped to the ground beside him, laugh cried, and gently set his head in her lap. She stroked the fur on his cheek, and then ran a finger along the soft spot from his snout to between his eyes. He could stay like that forever.

The beam of the light they were in grew more intense so that he had to open his eyes to see what was going on. *Helena?*

"It's not me doing it. I thought it might be you. Also...where did everyone go?"

Aleksei sat up, his bones healed, his mind clear, his soul intact. Even his wolf couldn't heal him that fast. Was it the power of love?

He looked up at his mate and saw a rainbow over her head.

Then a woman in white appeared behind her. "My mate and I can't thank you enough for your service to our children's future."

Helena looked over at the woman and shook her head. "We didn't do anything but love each other. Well, and kick some creepy old lady's butt. What's that got to do with your kids?"

The woman smiled. "I wasn't finished."

"Oh. Sorry." She motioned for the strange woman to continue.

"Love has conquered all, and it will do it again, but Chaos may follow behind," she said in a weird witchy way. The rainbow above their heads shimmered and a great multi-colored dragon landed next to the woman in white.

Oh shit. Aleksei had heard plenty about the troubles with dragons. He shifted and pulled Helena into his arms. He didn't want these beings anywhere near his mate.

"Why are you telling us this and being all cryptic to boot? We aren't a part of your war." Aleksei was starting to understand why Niko had such a mad on for the dragons. They were a giant pain in the ass.

Aleksei's tone didn't faze the white witch in the least, although her dragon gave him the stink eye. "Because I'd like to give you a gift in thanks for what you did here today."

Helena gave the stink eye right back. For being a human who knew very little about the supernatural world a week ago, she was handling seeing her first dragon pretty well. She should write a book for humans on how to deal with their kind or something.

"We don't need your treasure hoard or whatever. I've got all I need already." Helena squeezed his hand and his heart soared like the moon in the sky knowing she meant him. She too was all he ever needed in life to be happy.

"No." The witch gave little nod, acknowledging Helena's wishes. "I have something more precious than gold or jewels. I give you the gift of time."

Helena snorted. "Hmm. That sounds about as real as one of those gift certificates for a free backrub."

149

Aleksei kept his laugh in. He knew exactly what he was getting his mate for Christmas.

The woman placed a finger on both Aleksei and Helena's forehead. "When the war comes to Rogue, you will not see it, smell it, touch it, or hear it. Instead you will spend time loving each other."

The dragon shifted, and the man he became grinned like a loon and cleared his throat. "I've heard the humans have a thing called a kissymoon or something. Since she's a human and he's a wolf, that seems an appropriate thing for them to do while we're knocking things around with Ereshkigal and Kur-Jara in Rogue."

Helena, cross-eyed from staring at the witch's finger on her forehead, blinked. "You mean a honeymoon."

The dragon man thought for a minute. "That's the thing where you give each other lots of orgasms on a beach vacation, right? Then yes. Kissymoon makes more sense, unless you're into food porn. But I'm not kink shaming. You do you."

"Fine," the white witch said. "You'll go on a honeymoon so as to avoid fighting in our war. My sister and her revenge plans have already done too much damage to wolfkind, and if we can save even one life, then I'm happy to sacrifice two of their greatest warriors to a month in—"

"Oh, oh." The dragon got all excited. "Send them to that place in Thailand, what's it called, Fuck It."

The witch shook her head. "I think it's pronounced Phfoo Ket, not fuck it."

Aleksei looked deep into his lover's eyes and begged her to understand. "While I'd love to spend a month doing nothing but making love to my mate, I cannot in good conscience leave my pack to fight a war against the underworld."

Helena gave him a quick peck on the lips. "Same. Us girls can help too."

"Oh, the daughters will be the ones to turn the tide, should we be able to defeat Ereshkigal." The witch had way too many plans. "With this gift, I'm simply planning ahead. I'll need you two rested and ready. Even if we win this war, the battle between good and evil is never over. There will be more to fight for, I promise."

Helena sighed. "That doesn't sound ominous or anything."

"I'm afraid because your soul has been touched by the God of Chaos, he may try to use you again to come back and wreak his havoc on this realm. If my sons and daughters can defeat the Black Witch once and for all, Nergal will be weakened, but they're playing a long game here because she knows she cannot hold my eldest son's soul hostage forever." The witch looked over at the dragon. They both looked more worried than Aleksei thought beings with their powers should be.

This whole war was about a mother's love. It was hard for Aleksei to fault her for that. "So about that honeymoon. I'd like to start that sooner rather than later. I owe my mate a mating ceremony and tonight is a full moon, after all."

"I'll get the honey." The man winked and his body shimmered until he was nothing but a dusting of rainbow-colored flakes.

Weird.

"If that is your wish then you shall have it, brave warrior, and badass warrioress."

The next moment, Aleksei and Helena were standing in the center of the sacred circle under the light of the full moon. All their friends and family were there, smiling, talking, dancing, and making merry.

Helena wore a beautiful white gown and had flowers in her hair. She looked at Aleksei, and he wasn't wearing anything but a smile. "Hey, uh, weren't we...like a minute ago...umm."

"I don't know what you were about to ask, but I don't want to be anywhere else, doing anything else but making you my mate." Aleksei was moonstruck with how Helena glowed in the moonlight.

"Hey, you're glowing. Why are you glowing? I wanna glow." She touched his face and stroked his cheek like he was made of magic.

"You are, but I think only I can see it." The glow of fated mates. Selena had tried to tell them all that true mates would know each other. Undoubtedly, the matching fire for each other in their souls were alight, calling to join together. He had no idea it would make him feel like his heart was ready to explode.

"Ladies and gentlemen, wolves, and people of Rogue and beyond." Niko stepped into the circle and a beam of moonlight lit him up. "Welcome to our first open mating ceremony. If you think your fated mate is here tonight, step into the sacred circle and join with them. Everyone else, have fun."

"Ooh. This sounds like all official and stuff. What do we do?" Helena looked at Aleksei with so much love in her eyes he forgot how to talk for a minute.

Instead of words, he pushed the flowers and her hair to

the side and ran his teeth along her throat, right where he'd wanted to the first day they'd met.

"Oh my god. Do that again and I think I might come right here in front of everyone." She wrapped her arms around his neck and guided his head back to the same spot. "Whatever it is you're about to do, I want it. I want you, and I want the whole world, starting with all of our friends and, well, I guess half of Rogue is here too...I want them all to know that we belong to each other."

Aleksei wanted that too. He was eternally grateful that the Troika pack hadn't given up on him, even when he'd given up on himself. Because without them and their crazy revolution for love, he wouldn't have been able to claim his true mate and be truly, completely happy.

He pulled the gown off Helena's shoulders and found the neckline was stretchy enough that he could easily push the whole thing all the way to the ground, taking his time to caress her soft curves as he did.

"Mine." He licked the soft spot on her throat and gently sunk his teeth into her skin. Helena's knees gave out, but that was okay, he had her. Together, they dropped to the ground. Aleksei spread her legs with his, and she guided his cock to her wet folds. They joined their bodies under the moonlight and became one.

"I love you Aleksei Troika. You and your fantastic cock. God, I'm going to come from your touch alone. I want us to be like this forever. Don't you dare stop."

He would never stop. Never stop loving her.

Aleksei howled to the moon, thanking her for the gift of his mate. Other wolves in the sacred circle joined in the call and the forest was filled with the sound of love.

For the final time, Aleksei's wolf pushed him to mark his mate. It needn't ask again. He lowered his mouth to her soft skin, thrust his cock deep into her wet, willing cunt, and bit down. Helena's whole body locked and then spasmed with the first of what would be many orgasms.

I love you, zhin moya. *I claim you for my own and now you bear my mark for all to see.*

Helena's wolftress voice popped into his head. *I love you too, wolf man of mine. As soon as I come down out of this warm and fabulous place you've sent my mind and body, I'm going to bite you right back. Because if I'm yours, then you're mine and I want everyone to know.*

He would wear her mark proudly knowing together they would live happily for ever after.

EPILOGUE - NOTHING BECOMES SOMETHING

*D*eath.

   Despair.

Darkness.

That is all he had known for far too long. Although, he didn't have a good sense of the passage of time. Not since he'd died. Since he'd been killed. Murdered.

Betrayed.

He hid from the rest of the beasts letting his fur keep him warm, reveling in allowing his tongue hang out to taste the air, and waiting for his wolf to heal his new wounds. These woods didn't smell right. The trees were too new, the ground too warm, and the small, scurrying animals foreign to his nose.

This wasn't home. But deep inside he knew this was where he needed to be. He'd escaped the pits of hell, the monsters that lived below who'd used him as a toy soldier in their coming war, then cast him aside when he'd broken.

But once broken, he felt no more pain. Of course, he also

didn't feel pleasure either. His only consuming need now was to destroy the beast who'd betrayed him.

He'd been close. The woman and her mate had almost led the him to the dark one who called himself king.

The wolf he'd become knew what it was to be a king. That word didn't feel quite right in his mind. He'd been no mere ruler, on a throne, with a crown. He'd been the alpha of alphas, an emperor, the last hope for his people. The last of the Volkov Wolf Tzars.

If given the chance, he would have been a revolutionary.

He shook his head to toss away the cobwebs of his memory. He shouldn't even have this awareness, consciousness, or remembrances. He was dead. He was nothing.

Not nothing.

My mate.

My savior.

Help me.

The fur on the back of his neck stood up on end. Who had spoken into his head? He narrowed his eyes, scanning the night for signs of demons trying to trick him.

No telltale shadows wavered with their bat like lizard forms. No minions of evil, then. That was either good or very, very bad. If the Queen of Hell hadn't sent her wyrms after him, it must be either her pawn or her consort.

But no, the voice had been distinctly female. It asked for help from its mate.

A surge of lust rushed through his body as if his heart was pumping pure need instead of blood. How he would like to take this female and give her more pleasure than she could ever imagine, if only she would submit to him.

He would dominate her, protect her, make her his.

The heat of the desire turned to crystals of ice in his veins. He was no one's mate. Never again would he feel the thrill of having a woman under him. Death did not love and he was death itself now.

Despite the voice's protest, he was nothing.

In case the voice wasn't a trick by the inhabitants of hell, he opened his mind unlike he had since he'd been pushed from his former life.

I am not your savior. You must save yourself.

There was no reply to his harsh command so he closed his mind once again, locking it tight inside the shield of the wolf.

Tonight he would rest, heal, and consider the events of the past few days. He was in this strange foreign land for a reason. He'd scented old friends and foes on the wind and could only hope he'd been given the chance to seek his revenge on those that had betrayed and usurped him.

Tomorrow he would hunt again.

Somewhere not far from his hiding spot, he heard revelers mating under the bright moon. They came together in a sacred spot blessed by the Goddess herself. He wanted to watch, be a voyeur, but that world was no longer his.

He didn't belong there, he didn't belong here, he belonged nowhere.

Nothing.

Another presence shimmered into the darkness. Not a demon, or any other creature of Hell. This one could not contain its light. It sparkled like a million rainbows on the water.

He growled at the intruder. No one was welcome in his presence.

A man, with old injuries of war that had taken one arm, leaned against the tree across from the wolf's hiding spot. It emitted no scent of fear or even caution in the presence of a beast who would happily tear him to shreds and eat him for dinner.

The man chuckled and picked at a leaf. "I assure you, pup, I wouldn't taste very good."

Grr.

"I was like you once, you know. Knowing beyond a shadow of a doubt there was nothing in my soul. There was even a girl asking me to save her."

Your light is not like my darkness.

"Well, not now, you douchepotato. I got the girl and she saved me." His light flickered as if dancing or flying as he spoke of his girl.

I don't need saving. I am nothing.

"Ah, but we're counting on you to be something. Something very important." The last of the man's words faded as he shifted into a great dragon with multi-colored scales.

Fucking dragons.

———

FIND out what happens next in the Alpha Wolves Want Curves series with Filthy Wolf.

Can't wait for the next book in the wolf series? Check out the dragons! Get Dragons Love Curves here!

———

NEED MORE time with Aleksei and Helena - check out this bonus scene of their kissymoon - uh, honeymoon in Phuket, Thailand.

It's available exclusively to the Curvy Connection.

Already a subscriber to my email newsletter? Check for the bonus epilogue in your email!

Not on my list yet? Lucky you, I've got a free book for you and this bonus scene! Sign up to get both right now!

—> geni.us/MoreHungryWolf

A TASTE OF CHASE ME

*A*lways the Wedding Planner, Never the Bride

AGH. Ciara's feet ached, her back was stiff and the headache she'd staved off with some ibuprofen four hours ago was rapidly creeping back behind her left eyeball. Nothing like the sweet pains of victory.

One more commission like this and she could afford to take that beach vacation she'd been promising Wesley for the past three years.

"Oh Sarah, there you are." The bride's mother, who was reason number one, two, three, and forty-three for said headache, waved her over. Mother-of-the-Bridezilla paid the bills, so Ciara pasted on her most helpful smile and greeted the table.

"Hello everyone. Having a nice time?"

Headache mom turned to the couple sitting next to her. "Bill, Thi, this is Sarah, the wedding planner. You simply must book her for your Linh's wedding. She is the best—always available for her clients. I called her last week at two in the morning when I simply knew that Bethany needed to have three more wedding cakes at the reception. Sarah never says no."

Oh, great. That's what she wanted to be known for. Being the slut of the wedding planner world.

"Well, I like to hear that. We want our baby to have everything she wants for her wedding. No expense spared. Do you have a card, Sarah?"

"It's Ciara actually, and yes, of course." She handed Bill, who she could already tell was wrapped around his daughter's little finger, a card. Bill handed the card to his wife. "Let me write your time and date on the back for you."

She pulled a pen out of her kit. Always prepared, true to her Girl Scout roots. She scribbled on the back of the card.

"Ciara Mosley-Willingham. Do you own Willingham Weddings, dear?"

Sigh. Not yet. Not ever if her mother had anything to do with it. "That honor goes to my mother, Wilhelmina."

"Ah, I see. Well, nepotism has its benefits." The table all chuckled at Bill's little joke.

Benefits schmenefits. If only they knew.

"I've got an appointment that just opened up for two weeks from Monday. Will that work to bring Linh in for a consultation?"

"Two weeks?"

She nodded. "I'm afraid the next available is in August."

The couple glanced at each other. They were not used to waiting, patiently. Most of her clients weren't.

"That's almost three months from now."

161

Headache mother raised a glass of champagne. "You wanted the best. Better get her while you can."

Thi raised an eyebrow, trying to intimidate Ciara. Not gonna happen. Ciara gave the mother her award-winning account-getting smile.

Thi gave in. "We'll be there."

Bali with Wesley, here she comes. If she could ever get him to ask her out in the first place, and in another three years when her schedule cleared up. Not that her mother would ever allow her to take a vacation, but at least now she had a plan to get that date with the hunk of the office.

Ciara made her rounds, vying for a chance to run into Wes with the good news. News that should be celebrated, with a night on the town, a nice dinner, some satin sheets.

She checked in with the catering staff and found out he was in the kitchen. Wes, in a perfect three-piece suit with the purple pocket square and matching vest, just about took her breath away. How any man this good looking would be interested in her blew her mind.

By interested, she meant he flirted with her constantly at the office but hadn't ever asked her out. Ciara had made it perfectly clear she was willing and available.

He hinted, she smiled and nodded, and then nothing.

A girl could only wait so long for the man of her day dreams to make a move.

"Hey babe." He kissed her on the cheeks while holding his cell phone to his ear. "We've got a champagne shortage crisis on our hands."

No need to stress. Cool, calm, and collected. Always. "No problem. I'll bring in the secret back-up case I keep in my car."

Wes hung up his phone and winked at the disheveled waiter with the empty tray. "Told you Ciara would swing some of her magic."

He was such a sweet talker. She hoped he was a dirty talker too. Whoa, wait. Down girl. She had to get a date with him first. "I'll go grab it, but the bouquet toss is in a few minutes. Go chat up all the single girls and talk them into standing up to catch the bouquet."

One wink or an eyebrow waggle from him and they'd all be smashing each other in the face to catch those flowers whether they wanted to or not.

"I'll go get the champagne, you go catch the bouquet." Wes shook his head and shivered.

Lots of bouquets were in her future, but not for catching. Always the wedding planner, never the bride. Yet.

Here goes nothing, or something, or gah, just ask him.

"Hey, I just landed the Barton wedding. We should celebrate."

Wes grinned. "You are going to make us all zillionaires. I cannot even keep up."

Okay, this was going well. Ask him. "So, you'll go out with me to celebrate?"

"You bet."

He didn't hesitate even a little. She should have asked him months and months… and months ago.

"Are you free on Wednesday?" They had weddings on the weekends, but she hoped she didn't sound lame for suggesting a weeknight.

"Nope. But, I could do Thursday. Dinner, drinks, and I know the greatest place to go clubbing."

Dinner, drinks, and dancing. Perfect.

She wanted to jump up and down and clap her hands.

Not appropriate.

Be cool.

Ciara drew upon her inner cucumber-ness. "Sounds great."

Enough said. Right? Yeah, that was fine. She didn't want to look overly enthusiastic. She'd save that for the in-bed portion of their evening.

Geez, she needed to get her mind out of the gutter. She'd gone from dinner and dancing to handcuffs and blindfolds in seconds. Oh, please let him be at least a little kinky.

"Ciara?"

"Yeah?" She blinked, still caught up in her fantasy sex life with Wesley.

"You feeling alright? You look a little flushed."

She'd be fine and dandy if she could get the real Wesley into her fantasy life. "Yep. Great. Go grab that champagne and get it on ice."

"You're the best, you know that, right?" Wes grabbed her in a bear hug and danced her around. He jerked back and rubbed at his chest. "Ouch, your necklace bit me."

"Oh, geez. Sorry." Ciara put her hand over the colorful pendant she'd gotten a few days ago. She didn't feel anything sharp.

"Pretty but painful, doll." Wes examined the charm, staring a scant inch above Ciara's boobs. "It would go with everything. Where'd you get it?"

Damn. She'd kind of hoped Wesley had sent it. Not likely, but she was ever hopeful. Must be from her mother, who rarely gave gifts. Weird.

"Oh my god, Ciara, there you are. I'm getting a divorce, or is it an annulment? Whatever. George is such an ass. I want out of this marriage right now." The bride ran into the kitchen and faux collapsed into Ciara's arms.

She glanced at Wes, who shook his head and smirked. He mouthed the words good luck and backed away from them.

This woman wasn't the first newlywed to freak out at the reception and she wouldn't be the last. Ciara had a long track-record of calming them down and helping them focus on what was important, their happily ever afters. Wesley called her the bride whisperer.

Ciara put a hand on the bride's arm and sent all the happy calming positive thoughts she could muster. They took a deep breath together.

"You can do this. Everything is going to be fine."

The bride nodded, looking a little dazed and repeated Ciara's words. "Everything is going to be fine."

A few hours later, the bride and groom had more than made up. The bouquet was tossed, the champagne chilled and toasted, the candles blown out, all topped off by the perfect sunset.

At two in the morning, Wes escorted the last of the drunken groomsmen to the limos they'd arranged to drive the non-sober home and Ciara collapsed into the nearest chair.

If she took her shoes off now, they were never ever going back on, but she'd limp home barefoot rather than take one more second in her not-so-high heels.

A lonely uneaten piece of wedding cake had been calling to her ever since she saw the fit groomsman walk away from it several hours ago. After that marathon wedding and reception, she needed a good sugar fix.

"Stop right there, thief." The deep rumble of a male voice halted the fork midway to her mouth. Sounded like he was back for his dessert. Oh God. How embarrassing.

"I'm just doing a bit of quality control. Have to make sure the cake is up to Willingham Weddings standards."

Please don't let him mention the fact that the wedding was over. Ciara turned to give the groomsman her best don't mind me I'm just the chubby, dateless, wedding planner stealing a piece of leftover cake smile. The man-slash-movie-star-slash-romance novel cover model standing three feet behind her had his arms crossed and a mad as hell glare on.

He wore a tight black t-shirt, dark jeans and a beautiful bright green crystal on a cord around his neck, so he wasn't the groomsman, or any other guest of the Ketcher-Fast wedding. She'd remember all that fantasy material.

He glanced down at the glowing charm at his throat and stilled. He faltered for a second and had to grab on to a chair to keep his balance.

Great. Another drunk guest and all the limos were gone. No way was she driving him home herself. Hmm. Well, maybe. He was awfully sexy and all those daydreams she'd had about Wes all night suddenly starred this magnetic stranger.

Until he growled at her. "I don't give a damn about the cake, unless that is where you've hidden my goods."

"Your goods?" The only goods Ciara could comprehend at the moment were six, or maybe eight, of the most beautifully defined abdominal muscles in the whole Four Corners.

He crossed the scant yard between them in two strides, hauled her up out of the chair, and got so far into her personal space bubble she could smell his cinnamony breath. A zing whipped through her from every place he touched and strangely, she really wanted to stand up on her tippy toes and press her lips to his, taste that spice, lick up every essence of that erotic flavor.

She might have too if he'd held her for a second longer. But, after searching her eyes, he released her and began pacing, prowling around her, his eyes roving her from head to toe.

He might have the body of a god and she the body of a cupcake, but she would not be intimidated by wandering eyes. "First of all, you have to tell me what brand of tooth-paste you use, and second, back up out of my business, buster."

"Do not try to beguile me with your talk of hygiene products, your hair of gold, and your body made for sin. Where have you hidden my Wyr relic, witch?" He stopped circling and stared straight at her butt.

Body made for sin? Was he kidding? Body made of sins, maybe. Namely the sins of Swiss meringue buttercream, chocolate ganache, and too many I Love Lucy reruns. "Stop staring at my tuchus. Whatever you're looking for ain't in there."

She wiggled her backside to emphasize her point. That made her intruder damn irritated, probably that her rear wasn't dropping any evidence of wrong doing based on the growl rumbling from his chest and his eyes glued to her ass.

"Stop enticing me with your curves, thief. You cannot distract me from what is mine."

Ciara cleared her throat, gently at first, but when that failed to bring his eyes up to hers, she about gave herself a sore throat trying to get his attention.

"Are you ill? I won't have you dying before you tell me where the statue is hidden."

What an asshat. A cute one, but a real douche canoe nonetheless. "I think maybe we've gotten off on the wrong foot here." Ciara extended her hand to him. "I'm Ciara Mosley-Willingham." Her hand hung there for a full count of ten. "And you are?"

He recoiled from her hand. "Wondering what kind of spell you're trying to work on me. Whatever it is, I assure you a Wyvern is immune."

"I was trying to be nice, but I've had a very long and tiring day, so my patience is wearing thin. I don't have your thingy, and I don't know what a why Vern is. I thought for a minute I might help you try to find it, but I'm done now." Ciara turned and began looking for her torturous heels. It would be much more fun to stomp off if there was some clack.

"As am I. If you won't return what you have taken from me I will be forced to bring you before the AllWyr council."

"What the hell?"

He grabbed her hand and pulled her through the ballroom toward a terrace. Good thing she'd already kicked off her shoes or she'd have been tripping all over her feet at the rate he was dragging her away.

"Hey, stop right this instant or I'll bring out the self-defense moves."

"Save your defense for the council. You'll need it."

This dude was seriously a wackadoo. Where was the pepper spray when she needed it? Oh, that's right, still in the bag from the store her mother had insisted they buy in bulk from.

"Let me go."

"Return my relic."

"I'm gonna make you a relic."

"Save your spells, witch."

"Your face is a witch."

The scary man released her and grabbed at his face. When he didn't find anything wrong with it, he narrowed his eyes and glared at her. "Good try, witch. You'll pay for that."

Ciara pivoted and bolted weaving her way between the tables. One second she was zigging and zagging, the next she was airborne.

Great talons gripped her shoulders and a deep whoosh-whoosh-whoosh sounded above her.

She wriggled and screamed, frantically trying to see what was happening above her. Her feet crashed into empty glasses and caught a centerpiece of giant lilies dead-on as she was dragged through the air above the tables.

Before she could even take another breath to scream again, they swooped out of the French doors, over the balcony and into the night sky.

Ciara lost her effing mind as the ground beneath her sunk down into tiny squares of land. She couldn't look any longer, or she'd throw up. So instead she glanced up, not fathoming that she'd see flying above her the giant wings, flapping gracefully through the sky, of a dragon.

To KEEP READING - GRAB Chase Me now and get your dragon on tonight!

ACKNOWLEDGMENTS

Thank you so much to my writer friends who keep me going even during world disasters like Coronapocalypse. Extra hugs for Anna Michael, Sean Thomas, Dylann Crush, and ML Guida.

Without the Amazeballs, and the Amazeballs Writers sprint room I probably wouldn't have half the book written and would still be binge watching Great British Bake-Off.

Shout out to my Official VIP Fans!

Thank you so much for all your love and support for me and the characters I write. Your comments and messages inspire me to keep writing every day.

Hugs and Smoochies to you ~

- Dale W.
- Daphine G.
- Heather R.
- Jeanette M.
- Kerrie M.
- Frania G.
- Michele C.

And great big thanks to my Official Biggest Fans Ever. You're the best book dragons a girl could ask for~

Hugs and Kisses for you!

- Helena E.
- Alida H.

ALSO BY AIDY AWARD

Alpha Wolves Want Curves

Dirty Wolf

Naughty Wolf

Kinky Wolf

Hungry Wolf

The Fate of the Wolf Guard

Unclaimed

Untamed

Undone

Undefeated

Dragons Love Curves

Chase Me

Tease Me

Unmask Me

Bite Me

Cage Me

Baby Me

Defy Me

Surprise Me

Dirty Dragon

Crave Me

Slay Me

The Black Dragon Brotherhood

Tamed

Tangled

Twisted

Fated For Curves

A Touch of Fate

A Tangled Fate

A Twist of Fate

The Curvy Love Series

Curvy Diversion

Curvy Temptation

Curvy Persuasion

The Curvy Seduction Saga

Rebound

Rebellion

Reignite

Rejoice

Revel

By Aidy Award and Piper Fox

Big Wolf on Campus

Cocky Jock Wolf

Bad Boy Wolf

Heart Throb Wolf

ABOUT THE AUTHOR

Aidy Award is a curvy girl who kind of has a thing for stormtroopers. She's also the author of the popular Curvy Love series and the hot new Dragons Love Curves series. She writes curvy girl erotic romance, about real love, and dirty fun, with happy ever afters because every woman deserves great sex and even better romance, no matter her size, shape, or what the scale says.

Read the delicious tales of hot heroes and curvy heroines come to life under the covers and between the pages of Aidy's books. Then let her know because she really does want to hear from her readers.

Connect with Aidy on her website. www.AidyAward.com get her Curvy Connection, and join her Facebook Group - Aidy's Amazeballs.

Printed in Great Britain
by Amazon

79886600R00109